An Invaluable Weapon

"Oh my God," I said and clamped a hand over my mouth.

Tradd has hands the size of a catcher's glove, and he clamped one over my eyes. "Grandmother tried to warn you, Abby."

I yanked Tradd's hand away. "Just look at that kris! The handle is exquisite—the intricate working of the silver and superb quality of those apple green jade insets."

I know, I know I should have been ashamed of myself.

Sheriff Thompson went through the motions of feeling for a pulse. Of course, there was none to be found.

Praise for
TAMAR MYERS

"Professionally plotted and developed, and fun to read."
San Francisco Valley Times

"Rollicking!"
The Washington Post

Other Den of Antiquity Mysteries by
Tamar Myers
from Avon Twilight

GILT BY ASSOCIATION
LARCENY AND OLD LACE
THE MING AND I
SO FAUX, SO GOOD

BAROQUE AND DESPERATE

A Den of Antiquity Mystery

TAMAR MYERS

AVON BOOKS, INC.
1350 Avenue of the Americas
New York, New York 10019

Copyright © 1999 by Tamar Myers
Published by arrangement with the author
Library of Congress Catalog Card Number: 98-93546
ISBN: 0-380-80225-2
www.avonbooks.com/twilight

First Avon Twilight Printing: March 1999

AVON TWILIGHT TRADEMARK REG. U.S. PAT. OFF. AND IN OTHER COUN-
TRIES, MARCA REGISTRADA, HECHO EN U.S.A.

Printed in the U.S.A.

WCD 10 9 8 7 6 5 4 3 2 1

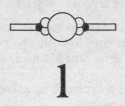

1

I dreamed the plane was hijacked by Yankee terrorists. It was horrible. They held guns to our heads and made us say the pledge of allegiance in under one minute. They took away our glasses of tea, and forced us to gulp gallons of diet soda. Then, just when I thought it couldn't get any worse, they tried to make us eat cornbread baked with sugar. Mercifully, I woke up before a crumb could pass my lips.

"You had a nightmare," the young man beside me said. "I didn't know what to do, so I poked you with my magazine."

I stared at him. He was handsome, too handsome for me to have missed when I boarded the plane. That's what happens when your cruise ship docks in San Juan on its final night, and you suddenly discover you have a taste for Puerto Rican rum.

"My name is Tradd Burton," he said, and gave me an easy, good-old-boy grin. "Tradd Maxwell Burton."

"Abigail Timberlake," I grunted. I do not dispense my middle name to strangers.

"You from Charlotte?" he asked.

I nodded, and my seatmate became a blur. There

1

was no need to ask where he was from. Tradd Maxwell Burton couldn't say the pledge in under a minute, even if he taped it and played it on fast-forward.

"You been on a cruise?" he asked.

"How'd you guess?"

"I saw the name of your cruise line on your bag when you put it in the overhead."

"You're very observant," I said, and closed my eyes. The young man had a right to be flattered. Usually I reserve sarcasm for close relatives and other people I care about.

"Hey, it wasn't one of those singles cruises, was it? I bet it was. A pretty woman like you . . ."

I said nothing. My head felt like a nut in a squirrel's jaws. I certainly wasn't up to flirting, even with someone as young and attractive as Tradd.

He droned while I drowsed. My best estimate is that I slept about an hour. When I awoke he was poking me again.

"You can stop it," I said. "I'm awake."

"Then put your seat forward in its normal, upright position. We're about to land in Charlotte."

I struggled to open my eyes. At some point my eyes had teared, running my mascara, and fusing my lashes together.

"Miss, I mean *now*."

I pried my right eye open with index finger and thumb. For my effort I was rewarded with a close-up of our stewardess, a battle-ax named Brenda.

You owe me six dollars for the drinks," she barked.

"I what?"

"When we hit that turbulence the captain asked us to take our seats, so I told your husband I'd collect later."

I glanced over at the seat beside me. It was empty.

I am vertically challenged—four feet nine inches, if you must know—so I didn't see Mama until the next-to-last passenger, a horizontally enhanced man, cleared my line of vision. Thanks to bellicose Brenda, who got another stewardess to swear she was a witness to the husband I never had, I had no choice but to pay for two phantom drinks. At any rate, Mama looked every bit as grim as Brenda.

"Oh, Abby, there you are!" Mama wailed and flung herself at my laden arms.

I hugged her as best I could. "There, there, I was only gone ten days."

"Abby, it was just awful."

"It couldn't have been that bad, Mama. You had bridge on Monday, church supper on Wednesday, and weren't you thinking of taking that karate class on Thursday? You said something about going for your black belt."

Mama struggled free from my embrace, almost knocking a bottle of golden rum from my hand. "You seem to be taking this awfully calmly, dear."

I pecked her cheek. "There. Is that better?"

"Is that all you have to say?"

I gave her the once-over. She is just four inches taller than I, so it didn't take long. Same full-skirted, fifties-style dress, pouffed up by a crinoline that she's worn for the last forty years. Matching pumps and handbag. Same permed bob, but with a slight blue tint now that she's in her seventies. No, there was nothing new to compliment.

"Mama, I really am glad to see you. Look, I brought you a gift."

Mama blinked. "A gift?"

"Well, nothing really expensive." I shoved a shopping bag at her. "The shawl is for you, the conch shell is for Charlie, and the I LOVE PUERTO RICO T-shirt is for Susan. But since neither of them is here, you can have first pick."

Mama recoiled in horror. "How can you stand there and talk about souvenirs when you've been ruined."

"Mama! I thought we agreed not to talk about my sex life. But if you must know, I didn't even *meet* a man that appealed to me. I certainly didn't sleep with one."

"You didn't get my message, did you?"

I felt my newly acquired tan drain from my face. "Is it the children?"

Charlie, nineteen and invincible, is fond of speeding in the Corvette my ex-husband gave him. Susan, twenty, is fond of older men. Twice she has given herself to the "only guy I'll ever love." Both my children are just a hormone or two away from disaster.

"Charlie and Susan are fine. It's your shop, dear."

"My shop? Was there a fire?"

The Den of Antiquity is my life, now that I'm divorced and the children are grown. Five years ago antiquing was just a hobby. Then one day Buford "the Timbersnake" Timberlake announced that he was trading in my forty-plus years for the forty-plus bosom of a twit named Tweetie who was all of twenty. Buford is Charlotte, North Carolina's most famous divorce lawyer, and has more connections than a telephone switchboard. There was no way I was going to get alimony, much less custody of my children.

So, I threw myself into my avocation and made

it my vocation. Some of it was luck, but frankly, most of it was just plain old hard work. Sweat equity, my friends call it. At any rate, the day I left for my much-needed Caribbean vacation, the Den of Antiquity on Selwyn Avenue was one of Charlotte's most prosperous antique stores, and I say that with all modesty.

Mama's fingers dug into my elbow as she steered me to a molded plastic seat. "Sit," she ordered.

My knees had no trouble cooperating with her command.

"You were burgled, dear."

"Burgled? What did they take?"

"Everything."

"The eighteenth-century soft-paste porcelain collection I got just before I left?"

Mama looked away. She didn't need to say anything; she was patting her pearls. Those pearls were Daddy's last gift to Mama before he died. She never takes them off, even to shower. Whenever Mama's nervous, she fingers those gems like they were worry beads. It's a wonder she hasn't worn through the nacre.

"Not the mahogany highboy from Philadelphia! Or the Jacobean buffet. They're both far too big—"

"Abby, dear, the thieves must have used a van or a truck. Even the cash register is gone."

"No, it's not, Mama. I locked it up in the storeroom. Of course, I don't keep cash in it when I'm away, but—"

"Abby, listen to me! They took *everything*—even your wastebasket."

I felt dizzy. I needed to lie down. I slumped lower in the hard plastic seat, but it wasn't the same.

"Did you say *everything*?"

Mama is a fixer. "Pull yourself together, Abby. You've started at the bottom before. You can do it again."

I fought back the tears. I hate making a public spectacle of myself, and Gate B19 at the Charlotte-Douglas International Airport was beginning to fill for a flight to Raleigh.

"You're right, Mama. I can do it again. Only this time I won't be starting from scratch. Thank God I remembered to give Susan the insurance check before I left."

Mama was shaking her head.

"Yes, Mama, I did. I was running late, but when Susan came over to say goodbye, I asked her to drop the check in the mail."

"Oh, Abby, if only it were that simple."

"Okay, so I forgot to send in the payment on time, and that was second warning. But all's well, that ends well, right?"

"Don't hate your daughter," Mama sobbed.

My hair stood on end. Fortunately, I keep it on the short side.

"Why would I hate her?"

"Remember, dear, that she's really not much more than a child. And she is sorry. She really is. She would be here right now telling you herself, but—"

"Mama, out with it!" I shrieked. Half the folks in B19 turned to stare at me, but I no longer cared. There comes a time when one must choose between decorum and sanity.

"Susan forgot to mail the check," Mama wailed, her face the color of marshmallow. "Your policy was canceled."

Mercifully I fainted.

* * *

I wasn't out long enough. Unfortunately, Mama is somewhat of an expert when it comes to swooning, and carries smelling salts in her handbag wherever she goes. She claims to have revived President Reagan when he passed out in Tokyo, but I say that's absurd. Since Mama has never been east of Myrtle Beach nor west of the Biltmore, I rest my case. At any rate, Mama thrust her vial of vile vapors beneath my nose and brought me rudely back to reality.

"What happened?" I purportedly moaned.

"Get a grip on yourself, Abby," Mama said, slapping my cheek, like it was a slab of yeast dough.

"What for? You were right, Mama, I'm ruined."

"Not necessarily. Perhaps I spoke too soon."

I sat bolt upright, causing a bolt of pain to shoot through my crowded cranium. "You mean this has all been some kind of sick joke? You mean I wasn't burgled?"

Mama's hand flew to her pearls, her one constant source of comfort. "Oh, no, you were burgled, all right. Picked clean. But who knows, Abby, some good may come out of this."

I stared at the woman who had gone through thirty-six hours of painful labor to bring me into this cruel world. She would have saved us both a lot of trouble if she and Daddy had never—well, never mind. Mama, I am sure of it, has never had sex. I am the product of a virgin birth, which just goes to show you history can repeat itself.

"What good can possibly come out of being burgled? Is Oprah doing a show on middle-aged businesswomen failures?"

"Oprah!" Mama clapped her hands. "I hadn't thought of her. That might be just the ticket!"

"Mama, I was just kidding. Oprah only does positive, inspirational stuff now."

"But, Abby, that's exactly what this is."

"For whom, the burglars?"

"Oh, Abby, you don't understand. This has nothing to do with the burglars. This has to do with your shop."

"Hmm, let me see. You want me to rent it to Oprah to use as a studio? Mama, it's a little small for that, don't you think?"

Mama had begun to twirl her pearls, always a dangerous sign. "Abby, are you going to stop being sarcastic and let me explain?"

Unfortunately fainting is not something I can do at will, and Mama's mind is like quicksand, the more you resist it, the deeper you flounder.

"Okay, Mama, tell me your plan."

"It's really very simple, dear. We charge admission—say, ten dollars a head. Although we might consider giving a discount to church groups and bus tours. The real money will come when we sell the book and movie rights."

I shook my head sadly. That's what I deserved for going on a cruise in July. Sure, Mama had always been a mite eccentric, but this was the first real sign of senile dementia. And to think I wasn't here when she might have needed me.

"Mama, it's you who needs to get a grip on it," I said gently. "People aren't going to pay ten bucks to gawk at nothing."

My dear mother was so far gone she laughed. "But they won't be gawking at nothing, silly. They'll be gawking at the . . ." Her voice trailed off and she pretended to look at a passenger with an ivory-topped walking stick.

"*What* will they be gawking at, Mama?"

"Oh, didn't I tell you?"

I grabbed her by the shoulders. "Tell me *what*?"

"Oh, nothing," she said, just to get my goat. It works every time. By now Mama must have pastures full of frolicking kids.

My right hand crept threateningly close to her beloved pearls. "Mama, don't force me to do something I really don't want to do."

Mama gasped. "You wouldn't!"

"Oh, wouldn't I?" Of course, I wouldn't! Not in a million years! But then neither did Mama mean those threats when I wouldn't eat my spinach forty years ago.

"There's an angel on the back wall of your shop," she said quickly. "It's the most astonishing thing I've ever seen. When you open and close the door, it flaps its wings."

I sniffed her face. "Mama, have you been nipping at the cooking sherry again?"

Instead of getting angry, Mama snatched up the shopping bag. "Just hush up, Abby, until you've seen it for yourself. Seeing is believing."

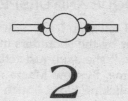

2

I stared at what remained of my shop. The Den of Antiquity was as empty as Buford's heart. Mama had not been exaggerating. All my carefully selected merchandise was gone, as was the cash register. Believe it or not, the thieves had even swept the floor; either that, or I kept a lot tidier shop than I remembered.

"See!" Mama said, pointing triumphantly to the far wall.

"What am I supposed to be looking at?"

"The angel, of course. Can't you see it?"

"No, Mama, all I see is a blank wall."

"Then get closer, Abby. The first time you see it, you need to be pretty close. After that, it just jumps right out at you."

Just to humor her, I trotted over for a closer look. It was my turn to gasp.

"Now do you see it?"

"Hey, I see a bunch of scratches," I growled. "And look at that gouge. Just wait until I get my hands on those burglars!"

"Those aren't just scratches, Abby. They're the outline of an angel. See, there's its left wing, and there's its head, and over there is its right wing, all stretched out." Her voice rose with excitement. "And see, in his—I can't tell if it's male or female— hand is a banner announcing the end of the world."

"Still just looks like a bunch of nicks and scratches to me, Mama. And that's not a banner, that's a scrap of newspaper."

"It says END TIMES," Mama practically shouted. "And in bold print. Abby, the writing is on the wall, and you're suddenly blind as a bat."

"I can see perfectly well, thank you. Mama, lots of the stuff I buy comes wrapped in old newspaper. And that's exactly what this is." I reached to peel it off, but Mama slapped my hand away.

"Don't you dare, Abby. This is a message from God."

"On newsprint? Mama, that scrap of paper is probably from the *South Bend Times*—or some other city with the same letters in its name. As for your angel—well, it was just the light playing tricks on your eyes."

"That's it! The light!" She scurried across the room and flicked on the overhead light. She returned panting. "Now look!"

I rolled my eyes and then focused them slowly on the illuminated wall. "Oh, my God!"

"It's not the Lord, Abby. It's just an angel."

"It's pure cheek," I wailed. "The burglars, damn their miserable hides, even took my phone jack!"

I thought Mama would jump out of her skin. "You mean you *still* can't see it?"

"Not even a feather. Now Mama, if you don't mind, can we please change the subject? I mean, here I am, standing in an empty shop—everything I own is gone—stolen—and you want to stand around and talk about fairies."

Mama's mouth opened and closed silently several time. Finally she managed to produce a few faint squeaks.

"What?" I said with remarkable patience.

The squeaking grew louder. "Not fairies, angels!"

"Just stop it!" I screamed. "This isn't about you, or what you think you see on the wall. It's about me!"

Mama drew herself up to her full five feet and one inch. "If that's the way you feel, then I'm going straight home."

"Goodbye, Mama. Thanks for picking me up at the airport, but I can take a cab home from here. Or hitch a ride with Wynnell or C.J."

She stomped to the door, angrier than I'd ever seen her. Well, the nerve of that woman! I was the one whose life had come unraveled, for crying out loud. I was the one facing bankruptcy.

Mama opened the door. "It's not too late to say you're sorry, Abby."

I gaped at her in disbelief.

"Well, then, I'm gone!" she said, and the door slammed behind her.

An hour later I was still gaping, this time at Inspector Greg Washburn. Take it from me, the man is a hunk; six feet tall, blue eyes, black hair, muscles in all the right places, which is to say, none between the ears. We were an item for a while, but I broke it off because—well, the truth is, we didn't trust each other. Of course Greg had no reason for his doubts, while everyone knows Greg had the hots for a bimbo named Hooter Fawn. I'm not saying he acted on his impulses, but I want a man who not only has eyes just for me, but who will kindly avert those eyes on a bad-hair day.

"I thought you were with homicide," I said.

"Very funny, Abby."

"It wasn't meant to be."

"You didn't know?"

I sat down on a floor so clean Mama could serve bridge-club cake on it and no one would complain. "I've been out of town. Or didn't you notice?"

"Of course, I noticed. I just thought that your mother, or some of your friends—never mind, it's a long story. Yes, I've been assigned to your case."

"Well, let the investigation begin," I said. Try as I might, I couldn't pry my peepers off him. I had tried dating other men—including a drop-dead-gorgeous detective from Pennsylvania—but it was no use. All I could think of was Greg, who seemed to have no trouble thinking of women other than me. If only there was some way to make him *really* jealous.

To my surprise, Greg sat down cross-legged opposite me. He pulled a small leatherbound notepad from the pocket of his navy blue shirt.

"As you can see, Abby, the person or persons who robbed your shop, made a clean sweep of things—uh, sorry, Abby, no pun intended."

"Can you tell me something I *don't* know?"

He shrugged. "We dusted for prints—there aren't any. No sign of forced entry. No evidence of a truck or moving van in the alley, although of course they undoubtedly used one. We even had a guy climb up on the roof—"

I waved my hand like a schoolboy with a right answer. We schoolgirls were far too polite to wave in my day, even though *we* had all the right answers.

"Wait a minute! What do you mean they undoubtedly used a truck or van?"

He closed the notepad and slipped it back in his pocket. "It was definitely a pro job, Abby. If I were to hazard a guess, the contents of your shop are halfway to California by now."

"*California?*"

He nodded. "I'm surprised you don't know. What do we have in the east that the Californians don't?"

I bit my tongue. There are plenty of Californians with sense. My brother Toy just happens not to be one of them.

"A hundred and fifty years of English colonial history."

"What?"

"We're talking about the resale of history, here, Abby. Apparently it happens with some frequency. Especially up north. I thought you would—"

I tuned Greg out. It had finally sunk in. The czarist samovar I bought at an estate sale in Myers Park last month, and hadn't even gotten around to pricing, was going to end up gracing the credenza of some Hollywood mogul. I found myself hoping that the purveyor of my stolen goods scalded himself where the sun didn't shine. Unless, of course, he or she was innocent, and especially not if he was Steven Spielberg. I'm still waiting for the sequel to *E.T.*

"I don't get it," I said.

"Damn it, Abby, don't you listen to a word I say?"

"Of course, I do."

"I just got through telling you that this was a professional job, possibly even part of a national ring. You're probably never going to see your stuff again."

"They were treasures, not *stuff*."

He nodded.

"How did they know I was going to be gone?"

"Maybe they overheard you talking to your travel agent, or one of the other antique dealers on this street. It could even have been someone from church. They're not all saints, you know."

"But they had a key, right? You said there was no sign of forced entry, and—"

"Where do you hide your key, Abby?"

"*What*?"

"Your key."

"Who said I hide a key?"

The Wedgwood eyes rolled impatiently.

"All right, but I don't hide it on a doorsill. Or under the front mat. I'm not that stupid!"

He sighed. "One of those fake stones you order through a catalog?"

"Of course not!"

"Show me."

I sheepishly took Greg to see the clever hollow brick I keep in the alley by the back door. It is much more subtle than those fake stones, and it's a real brick. I bought it at the Southern Home & Garden Show last spring.

But except for a rolled-up pill bug and a squashed cricket, the spot was as bare as Mrs. Hubbard's cupboard.

"Well—uh—it was there!"

"Abby, Abby, Abby, whatever am I going to do with you?" Greg shook his handsome head.

"Not a damn thing!" I stamped back into my empty shop, my very footsteps mocking me with their echoes. Greg trotted after me, adding to the mockery.

I was in no mood to see Jane Cox, aka Calamity Jane, standing in the middle of my display area. Given the circumstances, she was, of course, delighted to see me.

"Oh Abby, dear," she wailed, and draped herself over me like a flag on a casket, "it's just so awful. Is there anything I can do to help? *Anything*?"

I bit my tongue, which takes some doing in my case. As the mother of two college kids, I have permanent indentations in my lingual organ.

"Don't worry, Abby, my cousin Orville back in Shelby had the same thing happen to him, and it turned out just fine. You'll see."

I struggled free from her embrace. "Your cousin Orville had an antique shop that was burgled?"

"Gracious no, Abby. Cousin Orville dabbles in the future, not the past. He makes organic dentures."

Greg and I couldn't help but exchange glances. Calamity Jane—"C.J.," we call her—is as loony as a lake in Maine.

"Don't tell me he makes teeth out of ivory," I chided. "Elephants may be making a comeback in some countries, but—"

"Oh, no, of course not ivory. Cousin Orville Ledbetter uses pig teeth."

"And someone swiped his stock of sow incisors?" I asked incredulously.

Greg chuckled. "Perhaps the perpetrator was Porky."

"Or Petunia," I peeped.

C.J. gave us scathing looks. "As a matter of fact, the thieves were . . ."

The door to my shop swung open and in strode Tradd Maxwell Burton. Either C.J.'s voice trailed off, or my ears temporarily stopped working. As for Greg, the little vein on his left temple was now the size of Europe's chunnel.

Tradd Maxwell Burton was even more handsome when viewed through sober eyes. He wasn't tall as Greg, and was blond, rather than dark, but nature had certainly smiled on him nonetheless. Golden hair, golden skin, thick gold chain around thick golden neck, gold-brown eyes—everything about him was gold, except his teeth, which were milk white, and may have been artificial. They certainly weren't pig's teeth. At any rate, his shoes, socks, and polo shirt were as white as his teeth, and either he'd just stepped off a tennis court, or he made his living advertising bleach.

"Abby!"

What cheek to address me so familiarly in front of Greg. I loved it. Never mind that he'd stiffed me on those drinks. I'd wring his golden neck later.

"Tradd!"

He bent and gave me a quick kiss. The subtle scent of expensive cologne did not escape me. The stuff Greg wore came in big bottles and had one-syllable names.

"So this is the famous shop, huh?"

"*Was*," I said. "I've been cleaned out, as you can see." Frankly, I don't remember having mentioned to him that I owned a shop. Although, given my condition on the plane, anything was possible— well, almost anything. I am fairly positive I *didn't* join the mile-high club.

A sharp nudge from C.J. reminded me of my manners. "Tradd, this is Jane, Jane this is Tradd, and that," I said nodding at Greg, "is Inspector

Washburn. He's investigating the burglary."

C.J. cooed like an amorous pigeon. Greg grunted.

As well-bred as he appeared, Tradd responded appropriately. He cooed briefly, but not too flirtatiously back at C.J., grunted perfunctorily at Greg, and empathized deeply with my woes.

"Tell you what," he said, "I know just the thing to get your mind off what happened."

"I already ate a Snickers bar," I said.

He laughed and putting a golden hand on my shoulder, turned me so that I faced the front window. "Look out there."

"Oh, my God," C.J. squealed, "is that white Jaguar yours?"

Tradd fished a set of keys from the pocket of his tight, white shorts.

"And you're *giving* that to Abby?"

"Whoa, not so fast." He squeezed my shoulder. "Sorry, little lady, but this one is spoken for. I was thinking more along the lines of a nice long ride."

"Where to, Anchorage, Alaska?" C.J. was incorrigible. She was also grass green with envy, which, frankly, was a nice contrast for her apple-red lipstick.

"He's talking to me," I snapped.

"The South Carolina low country," Tradd said.

"You mean the beach?" C.J. wailed. "Man they were sure right about life not being fair!"

Tradd chuckled, obviously enjoying C.J.'s attentions. "Not the beach, exactly, although it's about eight miles away as the crow flies. I'm headed down to an old rice plantation just outside of Georgetown."

"I love Georgetown," I said.

"Abby, don't be ridiculous," Greg muttered.

I whirled. "Excuse me?"

Greg literally took a step back. "Georgetown is at least a seven-hour round-trip."

Tradd rocked casually in his white sport shoes. I'm not up on brands, but this pair looked like they might easily cost my monthly mortgage.

"Well, we wouldn't do it in one day," he said. "I had a weekend trip in mind."

Greg blinked but said nothing.

"Ooh, Abby!" C.J., I knew, would have been glad to shed eight inches and forty pounds just so she could crawl into my skin.

"A weekend trip?" I croaked. "Which weekend?"

"This weekend. I'm headed down there tomorrow. My grandmother is hosting a little treasure hunt and, well, to be frank, I need an expert's assistance if I'm going to play."

"What kind of expert?" Greg growled, and then seeing me frown, revealed his pearly whites.

Tradd smiled charmingly. In the war of dental brilliance, it was definitely a standoff.

"I need an antiques expert."

"Ooh," C.J. caught her breath, "I know almost as much as Abby."

I faked a patient smile. "Of course, you do, dear. But you have a shop to run. Whereas I . . ."

Tradd nodded encouragingly. "We play these games from time to time. It's a family thing, I guess. This time it's grandmother's turn, so she gets to set the rules. She's calling this one 'Find My Missing Antique.'"

"How bizarre," Greg muttered.

"Who is your grandmother?" I asked. Mama has some distant relatives down along the coast, whom she visits from time to time. Although Tradd and

I are clearly not of the same social set, Mama may have heard of his family.

"Grandmother is Mrs. Elias Burton Latham III," he said, the pleasure evident in his voice.

C.J. and I both gasped. We had just read an article on the Latham estate in *Architectural Digest*. Or was that *Art & Antiques*? At any rate, the article claimed that the Latham family maintained "one of the most significant collections of antiques in America today." I remembered that phrase, if not the magazine, because I fantasized for a week that Robin Leach burst into my shop with his camera crew and bellowed the same thing about me for all the world to hear.

"*The* Mrs. Elias Burton Latham III?" C.J. asked weakly.

Tradd shrugged modestly. "I suppose there could be another, but I don't know her."

Greg cleared his throat. "Let me get this straight. Your grandmother has lost some valuable antique and you want our Abby to come down and help you find it?

Our Abby indeed! Where was *our* Abby when Greg decided he needed to go grouper fishing down in the Florida Keys and ended up groping some groupies instead? And where was *our* Abby when Hooter Fawn cast her doelike gaze upon Greg's handsome features and I didn't see him for almost a week?

"Oh, no, she hasn't lost it," Tradd said, his voice as smooth as a California chardonnay, "she hid it. I just need to find it."

"How is our Abby supposed to help?"

"Well, since she is an expert on these things— you see, Grandmother won't be telling us what the item is. It's up to us to figure it out from clues."

"I still don't get it. What's in it for our Abby?"

I wanted to leap into the air and slap Greg silly, but breeding and geography prevented me. "Yes, what's in it for me?"

Tradd grinned, causing folks a block away to pull down their shades. "Well, besides the obvious—I mean, you know—I'll pay you five thousand dollars, whether we find the piece, or not."

C.J. clapped her hands. "Hot damn! You go, girl!"

It was definitely tempting. No, it was downright seductive. I would gladly *pay* to see the Latham estate—if I had any money, which of course, I didn't. But to be driven there by a handsome man in a Jaguar, *and* have the opportunity to spend two nights in those surrounds—well, it was all too good to be true. Don't forget that Mr. God's-Gift-to-Women had stiffed me for two drinks on the plane.

He seemed to read my mind. "Bring a friend, if you like." He nodded at C.J. "My brother Rupert is about her age, I'd guess, and he's flying in from Houston Friday afternoon. The two of them could make a team."

C.J. grabbed my arm and buried her nails to the quick. "Oh, Abby, *pleeeeeease!*"

"It's a very tempting offer, dear," I said reluctantly, "but five thousand dollars is one Federal sofa in so-so condition. You know that. It isn't going to restock my shop."

C.J. moaned.

Ginger-brown fingers raked back a shock of vanilla-icing hair. "Oh, didn't I mention that the winner gets to keep the piece? I'm prepared to split its fair market value fifty-fifty."

"No, thanks, Mr. Burton, I don't have time for games right now."

"Perhaps I forgot to explain that the minimum value of this piece is one hundred thousand dollars."

"Well—"

"All right, you drive a hard bargain. You can have the damned thing. After all, it's who wins that counts."

"That's very generous of you, but I just have one little problem."

"Would that be me?" Greg said hopefully.

I glared at him. "Actually, it's my cat, Dmitri. As you well know, Tradd, I've just come back from a cruise. Poor Dmitri has been penned up at the Happy Paws Pet Motel for five days, and I don't want to leave him there any longer."

"Can't your mama keep him?" C.J. cried.

"I don't think so, dear," I said crisply. "Mama is allergic to cats."

Tradd cocked a sun-bleached eyebrow. "Is that all that's keeping you from coming?"

"Yes." If it was indeed kismet, a kitty wouldn't stand in the way.

"Heck, then your problem is solved, because grandmother loves cats."

"She *does*?"

"She's absolutely passionate about them. Her last one—Mr. Tibbs—died last month. I'm sure she'd be delighted to see a new set of whiskers around the old place."

Broke and desperate as I was, it was finally an offer too good to refuse. "Okay, I'll do it. I'll go. But no hanky-panky, you hear?"

C.J.'s whoops of joy failed to drown out the sound of Greg slamming the door behind him.

3

Mama picked up before the phone could even ring. "Abby, is that you calling to apologize?"

I swallowed my pride. It was the first solid food I'd had all day.

"Yes, Mama."

In the ensuing silence permanent peace came to the Middle East, and Congress voted themselves a salary cut. "Then, say it, dear."

"I'm sorry, Mama."

"What is it you're sorry for, Abby?"

"I'm sorry for—uh—well—"

"You can't bring yourself to say it, can you, dear?"

I clenched my left fist and bit the bullet. "I'm sorry that I ridiculed you, and yes, I was too stupid to see the angel on the wall, although now it's just as clear as vodka."

"You're looking at it now?"

"Uh—yes, Mama." In for a penny, in for pound.

"Can you really see it, Abby, or are you just mocking me?"

I glanced around the room. I was at home, in my own little house where I live alone, except for Dmitri, my cat. I could definitely see *things*, just not angels.

"Yeah, I see it, Mama."

"But Abby, dear, your shop doesn't have a phone anymore, remember? It doesn't even have a phone jack."

"Uh—I'm using Tradd's cell phone."

Mama jumped on that before Congress could vote themselves a pay hike. "Who is Tradd?"

"Tradd Burton. His grandmother is Mrs. Elias Burton Latham III. Her given name is Genevieve. She has a place down there near Georgetown. Have you ever heard of her?"

I had to wait while Mama retrieved the receiver she dropped. "The name sounds familiar," she finally said. "Why do you ask?"

"Well, I've been invited to join the family for the weekend down there. Tradd wants to drive me down tomorrow."

"*And*?" Although Mama sings soprano in the church choir, she seldom hits notes that high.

"I'm thinking about it."

Mama sucked her breath in so sharply I felt the receiver press against my head. "You better think fast, dear, because you're getting a bit long in the tooth, and now that you no longer have a penny to your name—well, you get the picture. It isn't any fun to grow old alone."

"I thought you liked Greg," I wailed.

"Greg, shmeg—the man couldn't commit to his shadow if he had the choice. You take my advice, dear, and reel in the first good man to tug on your line."

"You mean I shouldn't follow your example?"

"Don't be rude, dear—you'll just have to apologize again. Besides, I'm beyond the age of romantic involvement. For you, however, there is still a glimmer of hope."

Somehow Dmitri, who had been rubbing against my legs, got his tail tangled in the phone cord. It took only a few seconds to extricate him, but during that time he caterwauled like a pair of toms on a backyard fence.

"What was that?" Mama demanded.

"What was *what*?"

"Abby, you're not at the shop, are you?"

"Stay away," I hissed at my darn cat.

"What did you say?"

"I said, of course I'm at my shop. I'm looking at your angel right now."

"Ah, yes, the angel," Mama said, thankfully distracted. "It's going to bring you good luck, Abby. You just wait and see."

"All the luck in the world won't put this Humpty Dumpty together again," I muttered, and then immediately felt guilty for being such an ungrateful and pessimistic daughter.

Oh, what a difference a day makes. Friday morning I woke up just as broke as I'd been when I went to bed, but I was much richer in spirit. Not only did I feel determined to climb out of my financial hole, I felt strangely optimistic about my chances of doing so. Perhaps *that* was the good luck Mama had predicted.

"Rise and shine," I said to Dmitri, who was lying on my stomach. "You and I are taking a trip to the coast."

Dmitri rolled over and purred, waiting for his chin to be scratched.

"Up, you flea-bitten feline!"

He yawned and then resumed purring. No doubt

I would have given in and scratched him into heights of ecstasy, had the phone not rung. As it was, I was lucky to take the call with my innards intact.

"Abby's Love Palace," I said breathlessly.

"Abby?"

I sighed. "Yeah, it's me, Greg."

"What the hell kind of way is that for you to answer the phone?"

"This is my house, dear. I can answer any way I want."

"What if I'd been someone else?"

I paused long enough for the Senate to eliminate pork from the legislative menu. "If you were someone else, odds are you wouldn't be grilling me like a weenie."

As usual, Greg misinterpreted what I said. "*Is* there someone else?"

"That really isn't any of your business, is it?"

"Damn it, Abby, you're not really planning on going down there with that guy, are you?"

"Give me one good reason why I shouldn't."

"Because you hardly know the dude."

"Bzzzz. Wrong answer—you lose." I hung up.

Tradd said he would pick us up at my house in Charlotte, North Carolina, but I told him to meet us at Mama's house down in Rock Hill, South Carolina. It was on the way to Georgetown, and I had a few things to straighten out south of the border.

Rock Hill is not only my childhood home, it's home to lovely and prestigious Winthrop University, where both my children are in attendance. I was driving down Oakland Avenue when I saw Susan sitting in the sprawling shade of a live oak tree in front of the Tilman Administration Building.

She was not alone, and from what I could see, her companion appeared to be of the male persuasion. I strained to see more.

It pains me to say this again, but it *is* therapeutic; my daughter has terrible taste in men. I suppose I am to blame for that. Just look at the example I set for her. It would be nice to blame it on genetics, but Daddy was a wonderful man, and so were both my grandfathers. No, it all goes back to that fateful day when I met Susan's father on a water slide, and didn't have the sense to realize that the slide wasn't the slipperiest thing around.

I found a place to park behind the music department and by the time I hoofed it around to the front lawn the young man was gone. I know his disappearance was incidental, because the second Susan looked up and saw me, her eyes grew wide as magnolia blossoms.

She jumped up. The one good thing her daddy gave her was six inches of height. At five feet three she towers over me.

"Mama!"

"Hey, Susan—"

"Didn't Nana tell you I was sorry? I was going to mail the check, I really was—"

I hugged her. I imagine a gazelle being hugged by a python has a similar reaction. We were, after all, in the open, in broad daylight, and I am her mother. At least the gazelle has a chance of escaping.

"Mama, don't," she gasped, "there are people looking."

That was nonsense, because at the moment we were completely alone, if you didn't count the couple intertwined next to the bushes fifty yards away.

Their eyes were certainly not on us. I let go anyway.

"I just don't want you getting away before I have my say."

She sat down glumly.

I sat cross-legged, facing her. "I'm not mad, dear."

"You're *not*?"

"No. These things happen. I forgot to mail my insurance in once myself."

"You *did*?"

"Yes, but—well that was a long time ago. The point is, I understand completely."

"You *do*?"

I nodded. It's harder to spot a growing nose on a bobbing face.

"I really was going to mail it, Mama. In fact, I was on my way to the post office when a friend asked me if I'd help him look up something in the library for a quiz."

"Is that the same friend you were talking to a few minutes ago?"

She turned the color of a ripe pomegranate. "Were you spying on me?"

"Of course, not, dear. It's just that when I drove up I saw you talking to a young man. Is he your boyfriend?"

"Mama!"

"Be coy if you want, dear. Just don't expect me to tell you about the hunk with the Jaguar who's taking me to the beach."

I seldom drink, I don't smoke, and I haven't done you-know-what for ages. One of the few pleasures I get out of life is shocking my kids.

"Get out of town! I don't believe it!"

"It's true, dear. Well, we're not going to the

beach exactly. But close enough. His grandmother has a house down near Georgetown."

"His grandmother," she said and sniffed. "Sounds like a lot of fun. Does he really have a Jaguar?"

"You bet. And a tan like you wouldn't believe."

"What's his name?"

"Unh-unh. You first."

She rolled her eyes. "Geez! All right, his name is Randy, and he's just a friend."

"Is he a student here?"

"Yes, he's a student. Now, can we drop him and talk about your hunk?"

I suppressed my urge to jump up and do a little soft-shoe victory dance. Or maybe burst into a rousing rendition of Beethoven's "Ode to Joy".

"Well, my hunk—his name is Tradd Maxwell, and—"

"Ooh, sick! Tradd Maxwell is too young for you, Mama. That's disgusting."

I felt as surprised as the python, had the gazelle hugged him back. "You *know* him?"

"Sure. He hangs around with my friend Caitlin. She's going to puke when she hears about this."

"Maybe it's not the same Tradd Maxwell," I said hopefully. "This one is blond, and wears a gold chain around his neck that could wipe out the national debt."

"Give it up, Mama. He's half your age."

"So you do know him?" I would have dug a hole and crawled into it, except that the venerable old oak had a plethora of roots and my only tool was a nail file.

"Stick to someone your own age, Mama. Somebody old, like Greg."

I told Susan I loved her, despite her poor manners, and that if she ran into her brother, she should tell him the same thing. The love part, I mean. Charlie is as selfish as any nineteen-year-old boy, but he is seldom rude.

Then, feeling like a balloon that has been deflated, chewed on by a slobbering puppy, and dragged through the dust, I went over to Mama's.

Mama opened the door wearing a pink dress with a full skirt pouffed to ballet proportions by a trio of starched crinolines. Since it was the week after Labor Day, her shoes were black patent leather. Her pearls, as always, were white. Judging by her outfit, it could have been any day of the week.

"Come in, dear, come in!"

"I can't, Mama. Dmitri's in the car and—"

Mama grabbed my right arm and yanked me into the foyer. "He's just a cat. He'll be fine if you parked in the shade."

"Mama, is that a pork roast I smell?"

She patted her pearls innocently. "I don't smell anything."

That was like the pope saying he'd never been to church. Mama can smell what her sister Marilyn is cooking for supper over in Atlanta, and that's a five-hour drive. She claims even to be able to smell trouble. I will admit to having a pretty good sniffer myself, but I am nothing like her.

"Mashed potatoes, pan gravy—black-eyed peas, and let's see, peach cobbler for dessert. Am I right?"

Mama shrugged, pulled me in, and closed the door behind me. "Please, dear, there's no reason for the neighbors to hear."

"Am I right?"

"You forgot the garden salads."

Unlike my mother, I have a hard time smelling lettuce across a room. "This better not be for me, Mama. I told you I'd be stopping by for only a minute."

"Everyone has to eat lunch, Abby. And besides I thought that nice C.J. could join us."

For a fact, Mama is fond of C.J. For some strange reason the two of them giggle together like school-girls. But this was not the sort of lunch Mama fixes for single women. This was her snag-that-rich-handsome-bachelor-for-my-poor-divorced-daughter special.

"So you have heard of Mrs. Elias Burton Latham III, haven't you?"

"Abby, dear, *everyone* in the low country has heard of Genevieve Latham. Old Money Bags they call her down in Georgetown. But not me, of course—I would never say such a rude thing."

"Of course not, Mama. It would be foolish to gossip about prospective bridegrooms for your desperate daughter."

"Why, Abby, how you talk!"

"Mama, don't you have better things to do than to meddle in my life?"

"Not a darn thing," Mama sniffed and headed for the kitchen.

The doorbell rang and I rushed to get it, but Mama beat me to the foyer. It's amazing how fast she can run in high-heeled pumps.

It was Tradd and C.J. He was just as handsome as ever, having ridden down from Charlotte with the top down—perhaps a bit more tanned even—but C.J. looked like something my Dmitri might have dragged in from under the back hedge.

"Hey, there," Tradd said, flashing his set of

pearls at Mama. "Is your mother home?"

"This *is* Abby's mother," C.J. said dryly.

Mama was beaming. "Come in, dear," she cooed. "I thought y'all might like a little lunch before y'all leave."

"It would be a pleasure, ma'am."

I glared at my progenitor.

"Sweet tea or plain?" Mama chirped obliviously.

"Sweet." Tradd's golden eyes were already busily scanning the living room, no doubt judging Mama, and by extension me, by her 1950s decor.

Mama seated us at the dining room table, Tradd on her right. C.J. on her left. I was, of course, at the opposite end, far out of kicking range. In all fairness, it was a delicious lunch and my mother behaved herself admirably until dessert.

"So," she said, adding an extra scoop of vanilla ice cream to Tradd's cobbler, "do you have any older brothers?"

"Mama, please," I hissed.

Mama turned and gave me a wide-eyed, innocent look. "Not for you, dear, for me."

Tradd grinned, sending roaches three blocks away scrambling for the cover of darkness. "No, ma'am. Just two younger brothers. Harold's married and Rupert is—"

"Spoken for!" C.J. looked like she was ready to tussle it out with Mama in the remains of the pork roast and mashed potatoes.

I wanted to die. "Ladies," I wailed, "you're embarrassing the man."

Tradd waved a bronze hand. Considering the weight of the gold tennis bracelet around his wrist, it was a wonder he could lift it at all.

"No, ma'am, I'm not embarrassed. I hear this

kind of thing all the time. Guess it goes with the territory."

"Is that so?" I crammed a spoonful of cobbler in my mug before I could say anything that would jeopardize my participation in the ridiculous treasure hunt his grandmother was hosting. It was no wonder Pretty Boy drove a convertible. A regular car couldn't accommodate his swollen head.

Three hours in a convertible may sound glamorous, but it is guaranteed to produce a month of bad-hair days. Thank heavens my dark hair is short, and reasonably manageable under normal circumstances. Poor C.J. was cursed with fine, dishwater-blond hair that she keeps shoulder length. Even by the time she arrived at Mama's she looked like she'd dipped her head in oil before sticking her finger into a light socket.

All that sun and wind is not kind to one's skin either. C.J. was as red as the ink on my bank account, and I could feel my own skin coarsen by the mile. I was beginning to entertain the possibility that Tradd Maxwell was really a sixteen-year-old boy under that tan, and Susan was on to something.

As for Dmitri, the poor dear had taken refuge under the seat before leaving Mama's driveway, and was clinging to the floorboard for dear life. Either that, or he had jumped out unnoticed, and was already soliciting a new mistress. I didn't have the nerve to check.

"Would you mind putting the top down, dear?" I wasn't about to look like a California raisin five years in advance of my fiftieth birthday.

"What?"

"The top!" I shouted. "Would you please put it down?"

Tradd grinned, shrugged, and pressed the pedal even closer to the metal.

It was pointless to argue. I cinched my seat belt even tighter and prayed that Jaguars didn't have airbags on the passenger side. I ate all my fruits and veggies as a child, so it is not my fault I am vertically challenged.

Just before we got to Georgetown, about six miles south of the junction of federal Route 701 and state Route 52, Tradd turned left onto a dirt road. The land was low and flat, the earth sandy. All around us were woods, predominantly pine, but with a notable sprinkling of magnolia, cherry laurel, and oak. We were still miles from the ocean, but already I could smell a change in the air.

The Jaguar slowed and conversation became possible for the first time since leaving Rock Hill. Tradd Maxwell was due an earful of words.

But before I could open my mouth, Tradd opened his. "I used to hunt in these woods," he said wistfully. "Deer, squirrel, possum—you name it."

"Bear?" C.J. asked.

"Well, not bear. But just about anything else."

"I hunted bear with my daddy."

"Killed her a bear when she was only three," I said.

C.J. poked me with an unnaturally strong finger. "How many points was your biggest buck?"

Tradd smiled, and the sun temporarily dimmed. "He was a twelve-pointer. Bagged him on my eighteenth birthday. How about you?"

C.J. clapped her hands in delight. "Sixteen points!"

"Damn! I didn't know they got that big. What kind of gun?"

It was time to jump back into the conversation, even though I know nothing about guns. "Shot me a twenty-pointer when I was only ten," I said. "Or was that a ten-pointer when I was twenty? At any rate, do you realize just how dangerous it is to drive that fast? Especially in a convertible?"

Tradd laughed. "Ah, that's just insurance hype. A convertible is just as safe as any other car."

"It's pickups that are really dangerous," C.J. said solemnly. "My Uncle Elmer, Aunt Mabel, and their seven kids died in the back of a pickup."

I turned to look at her. There were tears in her eyes.

"I'm sorry to hear that, dear. You never mentioned that before. Rear-end collision in Shelby?"

"Oh, no. They were hitching a ride in a pickup along the Broad River when there was a flash flood. They drowned when they couldn't get the tailgate down."

Fortunately for C.J. the estate of Mrs. Elias Burton Latham III was now visible through the trees.

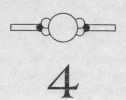

4

The Latham estate was built by slaves. It began as a rice plantation, a labor-intensive enterprise, and a 1790 census shows that Col. Elias Latham owned two hundred and eighty-five slaves of African origin, and four indentured servants from Wales, three male, and one female.

Colonel Latham was a particularly vicious man who raped scores of his female slaves, and the female servant, Mary Elizabeth Williams. When the latter became pregnant, Colonel Latham married her in the local Episcopal church, on New Year's Day. It was a short marriage, however, because on their way home from the church the couple was ambushed by a small band of slaves and the colonel was pierced through the heart by a wooden spear. The new Mrs. Latham was left unharmed, and much to the ire of her neighboring planters, did little to punish her slaves. To the contrary, it is said she ordered extra rations to be given all the slaves that day, and on the anniversary of that day for the rest of her life. At any rate, six months after her husband's death, Mary Elizabeth Latham gave birth to a son, Jonathan Elias Latham.

Two years after inheriting the colonel's estate, Mary Elizabeth Latham married one of the estate's white male indentured servants, Albert Burton. Rumor had it that she was pregnant again. Eight months after her second wedding Mary Elizabeth was delivered of twins, Elizabeth Louise, and George Albert Burton.

The two brothers were reasonably close, and Jonathan Elias Latham is said to have had an unnaturally close relationship with his half sister. Elizabeth Louise never married, but the foundling child her twin George and his wife took in, is said to have been hers. At any rate, in succeeding generations the Latham and Burton branches of the family tree have become more tangled than Rapunzel's hair.

This, then, is the American origin of the proud Latham-Burton clan, at least according to Mama. Apparently the Low-Country mavens are fond of reciting this family's history whenever scandal threatens their own. But despite—maybe even because of—the Latham-Burton's checkered past, folks look up to them. It is almost as if the colonel's clan has set a standard of eccentricity that society is still trying to live up to. The fact that the family has money is quite incidental, I'm sure.

The white plantation house sits on the left bank of the Black River. This body of water gets its name from its colalike water. The peculiar color is a result of tannin produced by the cypress trees that grow along the river's banks, and in some cases, well into the river itself.

"Ooooh!" C.J. squealed, "I always wanted to live in a house like that. How many rooms does it have?"

Tradd frowned. "Not enough. It looks larger than it is. You two are going to have to share a room, I'm afraid."

I prayed that my sigh of relief wasn't audible. I had *assumed* Tradd knew better than to presume upon my good character. Just because I am a divorcée, does not make me a tramp.

"That's okay," C.J said, "even though Abby snores."

"I do not!"

"But you do—you sound just like a cement mixer."

I glared at her. "Who are you to talk?"

"But, of course, you can't help it, Abby. Lots of people who drool in their sleep snore as well."

"C.J.!"

Tradd pretended to ignore our tiff and gallantly opened our doors. "Well, ladies, shall we disembark? Grandmother is undoubtedly waiting for us in the drawing room."

C.J. and I tumbled eagerly out of the car. It felt good to stand again—although frankly, I was the only one who didn't need to stretch his or her legs. C.J. did a curious one-legged hop, followed by a series of jumping jacks, and ended by swinging her arms in circles like propeller blades. Tradd, on the other hand, stretched and yawned just like a cat.

"Oh, my gosh! Dmitri!"

I dove under the front seat and was rewarded for my heroism by a hiss. I recoiled in shock. My beloved fur ball has never scratched, bit, or hissed at me. His vet, however, is missing a pinky nail.

A few seconds later I tried again. This time he not only hissed, but the claws on his right paw grazed the tip of my nose.

Although not in physical pain, I was nonetheless

deeply hurt. "Don't you take a swipe at Mama! Do you hear me?"

Dmitri growled.

I stood up, baffled and defeated.

"Anything wrong?" Tradd asked gently.

"I think you traumatized him by driving too fast," C.J. said before I could stop her. But she was absolutely right.

Tradd grinned. "Sorry. You think he'll be all right?"

I shrugged. "Does your grandmother have dogs?"

"Not a one."

"Any in the neighborhood?"

Tradd waved his arms at the surrounding woods. "I wouldn't think so."

"Then I'll just let him be for a while. Give him a chance to calm down."

"You sure?"

I was pretty sure. Cats might act like they're not paying attention most of the time, and they're certainly less responsive than dogs, but they have a sixth sense that is positively uncanny. I wouldn't be surprised if Dmitri was able to find his way back to Charlotte, even though he hadn't laid eyes on even an inch of road. Certainly he was capable of following my trail to the house. Or was he? Any animal that chases his own tail has got to be spatially challenged.

"We can check on him frequently," C.J. said and patted my arm.

I left a handful of cat treats beside the seat and poured some Evian in his bowl. "See you later, guy." I turned to the others. "Well, I'm ready."

"Then, let's go," Tradd said and offered us each an arm.

I am ashamed to say that for the next few minutes I forgot all about Dmitri. If only I hadn't agreed to bring C.J.

"Ooooh, look at all these cars," she squealed. Believe me, the woman drools just as much as I do.

I looked. Parked beneath spreading, moss-draped oaks, were a Ferrari, another Jaguar, a Cadillac, a Mercedes, and a Rolls-Royce.

"I guess we're the last ones here," Tradd said, rubbing his golden chin. He sounded disappointed.

"Who drives the Ferrari?" C.J. asked shamelessly.

"That would be my brother Harold. His wife Sally drives the blue Jag. She claims Hal drives too fast."

"Perhaps it's genetic," I mumbled.

"Excuse me?"

"The Caddie, dear. I was talking about the Caddie. My ex-husband Buford gets a new one every year. Trades it in at Arnold Palmer Cadillac in Charlotte."

"Yeah? Well, that old clunker belongs to my cousin Alexandra Latham. It's got to be at least five years old."

"You don't say! Well, personally I'd go for that pearl-gray Mercedes over there—I mean if I had the money. It's almost the same color as that clump of Spanish moss hanging above it."

"That belongs to Albert Jansen, my brother-in-law. My sister, Edith, had her own, but she wrapped it around a palm tree on a miniature golf course at Myrtle Beach."

"Was she all right?"

"Fine as frog hair. Not a scratch on her—but the car was totaled. The owner of the course bought it and left it right where it was. Now when you want to play the ninth hole you have to putt around the damn thing."

"Which leaves the Rolls," C.J. said. "Your grandmother's?"

Tradd laughed. "Actually that belongs to Flora, Grandmother's maid."

"Get out of town," I said, borrowing Susan's phrase.

"Yeah, well, Grandmother doesn't drive anymore, and Flora does all her errands. I guess it makes sense. Anyway, it's Grandmother's money."

"For sure. Believe me, *when* I come into money again, and if I live to a ripe old age, I'll dispense my goodies as I so please. My children are both sound of body and mind, and as such, need to make their own way in this world. I certainly don't expect to inherit Mama's money."

The truth is, I had no idea what the total of Mama's assets might be. Daddy was a traveling salesman for a Rock Hill clothing mill, and couldn't have made a whole lot of money. Mama, I know, has never worked outside her home a day in her life, yet she seems relatively comfortable. When I got home I was going to have to ask her about her finances. For her sake, mind you, not mine.

"Well, ladies, shall we?" Tradd asked, and gestured toward the house.

We followed him up the leaf-strewn walk to what looked like Tara on stilts. The Latham mansion, like many in the area, sits well off the ground, an accommodation to floods and the periodic hurricane. In the old days the space under the porch would have offered shelter to chickens and dogs, maybe even slaves, in a thunderstorm. Now it was home to a rusted old Chevy, which had once been the color of asparagus soup. Call me a snob, but *that* car sure didn't fit the picture.

"That's cook's car," Tradd said, reading my mind. "Grandmother insists she park it out of sight." He rang the bell with a golden thumb. "I hope y'all like planter's punch," he said with a wink.

The door swung open immediately to reveal a young woman in full maid's uniform. I took an immediate dislike to her. For one thing, she was a lazy, bottle blonde—inch-long licorice roots betrayed her. For another thing, she was far too made-up for that hour of the day. Even a geisha wears less foundation, for crying out loud. And those cheeks! The bright pink circles dusted on them looked like they'd been put there by a clown—either that, or she was burning up with fever. Furthermore, she was one of those types whose legs don't quit until they hit the armpits. The woman's inseams were longer than me!

"Hey, Flora," Tradd said.

"Hey, yourself," she replied.

Tradd ushered us past Flora without introductions. The entrance hall ran almost the full length of the house, and was as wide as my living room at home. Pairs of narrow, straight-backed mahogany benches flanking the walls faced each other. Above them hung portraits of ancestors who seemed more angry than inbred. A trio of threadbare carpets, lying end to end, were the only ornamentation. I guessed from the uncommon use of bottle green that they were Kazak rugs from Turkey. Still, it was an austere decor, more befitting a Mennonite innkeeper than a Low-Country aristocrat.

At the end of the hall Tradd pushed open a

heavy wooden door and I gasped. There, in front
of my wind-dried eyes, was the finest collection of
eighteenth-century English furniture I had ever
seen in one room. No doubt the colonel had it all
shipped over from the old country when he built
the house.

"Pinch me," I whispered to C.J.

She obliged.

"Stop it!"

"Abby—"

"What!" I snapped.

C.J. was rolling her eyes like bingo numbers in a
tumble wheel.

Then I noticed that several of the pieces of furniture were occupied by people. I gasped again.
Funny that I should have noticed the antiques first,
even though one of the room's occupants was almost as old as the chair upon which she sat.

"Grandmother," Tradd said, inclining his golden
head slightly, "I would like you to meet Abigail
Timberlake and Jane Cox. Abigail is going to be my
date for the weekend, and Jane will be Rupert's. I
spoke to you about them on the phone, remember?"

The men present rose to their feet.

Meanwhile, the grande dame and I gave each
other the once-over. She had undoubtedly known
God when he was a boy. Her skin was paper thin,
and where it wasn't pulled tight and translucent
against bones, it hung in neat folds, like Mama's
parlor drapes. What remained of her white hair
was brushed in wisps toward the center of her
head and tied with a black velvet ribbon that
matched her black velvet dress. No doubt she had
once been a very tall woman, because she was tall
even now in her dotage, her posture ramrod

straight. Her eyes, however, were timeless. They reminded me of the parrot my Aunt Marilyn used to have—glittering buttons that hinted at intelligence, but when the head turned became flat and inscrutable.

"Hello," I said, and took the old lady's hand. It was as light and dry as a biscuit.

"Hey," C.J. said, and did a silly little curtsy.

Mrs. Elias Burton Latham III had a voice like gravel in a tin cup. "Welcome to Latham Hall Plantation. I trust my grandson didn't scare the wits out of you entirely by the way he drives."

"Grandmother!"

The old lady pointed a bony finger at Tradd. "That boy's a menace on the roads. I've told our sheriff not to look the other way, just because he's a Burton. A little time in jail might do him some good—well, never mind all that now. I suppose Tradd has already told me, but where are y'all from?"

"Rock Hill, ma'am." I felt like I was in fourth grade again.

"I'm from Shelby, North Carolina," C.J. said proudly.

Mrs. Latham frowned. "Some things can't be helped, child. Anyway, I want y'all to meet the rest of the family. This—" she patted the arm of a ravishing redhead beside her, "is my granddaughter, Alexandra Latham. They call her Andie, but don't y'all dare."

"No, ma'am," we promised.

"Hello," Alexandra said softly. "It's a pleasure to meet you."

I, for one, wanted to gag. Alexandra was the perfect late-twentieth-century southern belle. Physically she was flawless, from her straight teeth to

the tips of her pedicured toes. Each auburn hair
was in place, and her periwinkle eyes neither
needed nor received any makeup to enhance them.
The last skin I saw that smooth and white was on
a baby's bottom.

From those few words she had spoken I could
tell she had perfect diction, perfect manners, and
no doubt carried within her ovaries the perfect
eggs to produce the perfect children. Still, she
wasn't married, was she, so how perfect could she
be?

I smiled warmly. "Howdy, ma'am."

C.J. curtsied again.

The old woman beamed with approval. "Now
that"—she pointed to a woman across the room—
"is my granddaughter, Edith Burton Jansen."

While Edith and I exchanged mumbled greet-
ings, I gave her the once-over. She looked nothing
like her brother Tradd. A coarse, broad-faced
woman, she exuded none of his sunshine, although
she had obviously spent her life in the sun. She had
one of those baked-in tans that had turned her skin
into creased leather. And she was brown, not
golden. Everything about her was brown, her eyes,
her hair, even her lipstick was one of those awful
earth tones briefly popular in the seventies. Tall,
like her grandmother, but chunky, she was
squeezed into a beige dress two sizes too small. I'll
say this, for her, however, she did have good taste
in jewelry. Her diamond ear studs were set in
white gold, and just large enough to grab my attention without turning me green with envy. It was
the pear-shaped pendant that turned me into a
four-foot-nine-inch avocado.

"Edith is the oldest of the lot—"

"Grandmother!"

Mrs. Latham cocked her head, a smile playing at her thin lips. "There is no shame in being old, dear. There is only shame in acting old before one's time. You know," she said, turning to me, "I've outlived both of my children. *That* is the real downside of attaining my age. How old do you think I am, dear?"

I shrugged. I have always been bad at guessing ages, and since most southern women would rather reveal their waist size than their true age, I was not about to take a chance and perhaps mortally offend our hostess for the weekend.

"How about you, child?" the old woman said, fixing her parrot eyes on C.J. "Would you like to guess?"

"One hundred and two," C.J. said without hesitation.

The National Weather Service could have named a hurricane after the collective gasps in that room. Mrs. Latham, however, chuckled.

"I like your candor, child. So I look that old, do I?"

C.J. nodded. "No disrespect, of course. It's just that my great-aunt Melva turned one hundred last week and she looks two years younger than you."

The avian eyes twinkled. "I'm eighty-nine, child. I'll be ninety on Christmas day."

"I'm sorry, ma'am," I muttered.

The bony hand waved away my apology. "That stuffy-looking gentleman sitting next to Edith is her husband, Albert. He's an engineer at Georgetown Paper. This may surprise you, but he's the only one in this room with a college degree—unless, of course, one of you two can make that claim."

"I have a bachelor's degree," I said reluctantly.

"Good for you, dear, but I'm afraid our Albert

has you beat. He has a doctorate of something or another. What is it you have your degree in, Albert?"

Albert said something unintelligible.

"Speak up, man."

"Chemical engineering," Albert said. He looked as happy as a cat in a drizzle. I felt sorry for the man. He was plump and balding, much shorter than his wife—although of course taller than me— and wore round wireless spectacles. He lacked the polished edge that only old money can buy. I think he would have preferred to be sitting in a Quonset hut somewhere having his fingernails pulled out.

"That's right, our Albert works with chemicals. Now Harold, over there"—the claw pointed to the right corner of the room—"almost got his degree in literature. Yale University, if you can imagine that. But wouldn't you know our Harold preferred good times over study. Isn't that right, Harold?"

Harold nodded. He was an older version of Tradd, not so golden—a few extra years of sun and wind had done their job—but not as brown as their sister.

"Harold doesn't have a job, but he does have a title. He likes to call himself an investment planner."

"Grandmother Latham, please—"

"Ah, and this lovely woman is his wife, Sally. She's an Armstrong, but she does have a drop or two of Latham blood. Don't you, dear?"

"Well, yes, but—"

"Ah, yes, that's right, her dollop comes from the wrong side of the blanket, but then again, so do most of great-great-granddaddy's descendants. I, in fact, brought more Latham blood to my marriage than did my husband, Elias. But then, our Sally here, brought something besides."

"Grandmother!" Harold said with surprising sharpness. "Sally's business affairs are a private matter."

"Then keep them that way and quit asking Grandmother for money," Edith said, her lips barely moving.

The crone smiled, her mission accomplished.

I felt sorry for Sally Armstrong Burton. She was a pretty woman about my age, with large blue-gray eyes, and natural blond hair—believe me, I can always tell these things. At any rate, she seemed to be the type of woman who, under better circumstances, would have been mildly perky and fun to be around. I decided to come to her rescue.

"And that must be Rupert," I said, gesticulating at the youngest male in the room.

"Yes, yes, the baby in the bunch. Our wee little Rupert Burton. Rupert, tell our guests what you do for a living."

Rupert turned the color of a rutabaga. It was not an attractive hue on him, especially since there was so much of the man to be seen. His head was shaved, and his short-sleeved powder-blue silk shirt was open practically to the navel. He was wearing baby-pink shorts and leather-thonged sandals. On the plus side, he had a gold earring in his right ear, and a cleft in his chin deep enough to cause an echo.

"I park cars for the rich and famous," he said at last.

My heart skipped a beat. "In Beverly Hills?"

"Yeah."

"It wouldn't happen to be at a restaurant called Fallen Stars, would it?"

"Yeah. Tradd tell you?"

"No, it was a lucky guess. That's where my brother Toy works. Do you know him?"

"Toy—nah, I don't know no one by that name."

"Don't know *anyone*," Mrs. Latham rasped.

"Yeah, Grandmother, that's what I said."

"But I'm sure my brother works there. He doesn't look a thing like me—he's tall, blond, really good-looking."

"You're not so bad-looking yourself."

"Abby, stop flirting," C.J. whined, "he's supposed to be my date for the weekend."

Mrs. Elias Burton Latham III frowned. "Sit," she commanded.

We sat. C.J. and I sat on eighteenth-century walnut armchairs covered in original petit point floral needlework. Tradd lowered his keister to a Chinese Chippendale-style chair that might have come straight from the Brighton Pavilion. The other men took their seats as well.

The grande dame gave us a satisfied smile and rang a small brass bell. Mama has one exactly like it, in the shape of a southern belle dressed in a bonnet and hoop skirt.

"Now that everyone is here," she said, "let the games begin."

5

The door to the parlor opened and in flounced Flora, she of the unending legs. In her arms, looking like he'd just swallowed a canary, was Dmitri.

"Look what I found by the front door," she announced.

"Dmitri!" I rushed over to rescue him.

Flora swiveled away from me. "Hey, take it easy. This isn't your cat."

"Yes, it is."

"No, ma'am, I found him outside the front door. He was crying his little heart out."

I lunged for my sometime bundle of joy, but missed. I lunged again. This time I was at least able to touch him. Unfortunately, Dmitri snarled.

"You see? He doesn't even like you."

"He's mine just the same."

"No, he's not."

"He is," Tradd said.

Mrs. Latham coughed to get our attention. "Tradd, is that the cat you were telling me about?"

"Yes, Grandmother."

Ten years seemed to drop from her face. "Bring him here."

Flora meekly allowed Tradd to relieve her of Dmitri who, in turn, meekly allowed Tradd to carry him over to Mrs. Latham. Dmitri couldn't seem to leap into the old lady's arms soon enough."

"Well!" I said.

"He nearly scratched her face off when she tried to get him out of the car!" C.J. would rather tattle than breathe.

Mrs. Latham who was already stroking Dmitri with her right hand, waved Flora out of the room with her left. "Don't worry about it, child," she said to me. "That's what makes him a cat. He's angry at you for something, and he's determined to make you pay. But he'll soon forgive you, and be back in your arms purring up a storm. Would you mind terribly if I hold him until then?"

"Knock yourself out, ma'am."

She beamed. "How old is he? Tell me all about him."

Lord knows I tried to, but I hadn't gotten much past Dmitri's weaning when Flora reentered the room, unbidden as you might have guessed. I glared at her, but no one else seemed to mind. She was, after all, balancing a tray with ten tall drinks on it.

"Planter's punch," Tradd whispered, but loud enough for the woman to hear. "Flora makes the best in the county."

"Is that so?" I said. I really didn't mean for it to sound quite as sarcastic as it did.

The faux French maid approached me first. "Care for a punch?"

"Why, yes, dear, I'd love one."

When she bent to place a glass in my outstretched hand, her bosoms billowed forward, threatening to burst from the confines of the black, maid's uniform and smother me.

"Slut," I said to myself.

When she bent to serve Tradd's brothers across the room, I saw her matching black panties.

"Tacky, tacky," I said to myself. I swear, my lips did not move.

"Flora has her faults," Mrs. Latham said, reading my mind, "but she's reliable. That's more than you can say about most folks these days."

The tramp in question turned and flashed me an insolent grin.

"I've never had planter's punch before," I said coolly. "It's very good."

"This was my Elias's recipe."

"It's very good," C.J. agreed. "Much better than my Uncle Willie's pollywog punch."

Foolishly, the matriarch bit. "I never heard of pollywog punch, child. What's in it?"

"Vodka, vermouth, a little lime juice, and, of course, pollywogs."

"C.J.!"

Much to my surprise, Mrs. Latham smiled. "Perhaps you'll be so kind as to give Flora the recipe."

"Ooh, I'd love to. And maybe she'd like my great-aunt Calmia's recipe for toad-in-the-hole."

"It's an authentic English dish," I explained to Mrs. Latham. "C.J.'s made it for me before. It's really quite good."

C.J. frowned. "Did I serve you my Aunt Calmia's version of toad-in-the-hole, or the English one, Abby?"

"What difference does it make?" I said through gritted teeth.

"My Aunt Calmia was born and raised in Shelby. She uses real toads."

I gagged. Tradd gallantly patted my back. When I was quite through trying to bring up the remains of Mama's lunch, our hostess spoke again.

"The rules of this weekend's event are quite simple"—she paused, allowing the black buttons to settle on us briefly—"you see, my dears, my grandchildren and I are very fond of games. Aren't we?"

"Yes, Grandmother," Edith said.

"That last one was Edith's doing," Mrs. Latham said. "A scavenger hunt to the Bahamas."

"It was beastly hot," Rupert whined. "Freeport in July is not my idea of a good time."

"You won, didn't you?" said Albert.

"Yeah, I won."

"Because if you didn't like the prize—"

"I liked the prize."

"You damn well better have. That Porsche cost me a pretty penny."

"You mean it cost Edith, don't you?"

"You son of a—"

"Albert!" Edith said sharply.

The auburn-haired Alexandra came softly to the rescue. "When it was my turn, I chose a mystery cruise of the Mediterranean. There weren't any prizes, just surprises."

"Like the belly dancer in our Cairo suite!" Sally said. "Unfortunately, she wasn't a real belly dancer, but a stripper. I was off shopping when Harold discovered her, and by the time I returned Fatima was down to her last veil."

Husband Harold turned red and grinned. "Grandmother, weren't you about to explain your rules?"

"Ah, yes, thank you, dear." Mrs. Latham surveyed her descendants slowly, adding to the drama. "First, as you know, this is a treasure hunt, and first prize is one of my antiques."

There were a few groans, and I think I recognized Rupert's voice.

The old lady held up a quieting hand. "But, as I said on the invitation, that missing antique is worth a minimum of a hundred thousand dollars—which, I believe, is still worth more than a Porsche. Not that a Porsche isn't prize enough for a family game."

Albert raised his glass of punch. "Touché."

Flora must have slipped out and in again, unnoticed, because suddenly she was at my elbow with a silver tray of shrimp canapés. I decided to compliment the cook and took several.

When we were all served, the grande dame cleared her throat. "Now, here are the rules. You may play individually, or as teams." She glanced at C.J. and me. "Some of you have decided to bring professionals into the game. That is fine, too. I believe I said so on the invitation."

"You did," Sally said, "but Harold and I don't need one, that's for sure. And I doubt if Edith and Albert do, either."

Edith scowled at her sister-in-law. "Speak for yourself."

The bird eyes brightened. "The game begins now and continues until three o'clock Sunday afternoon, *or* until the missing antique is found. However, between the hours of midnight and eight in the morning, both tonight and tomorrow night, the game will be temporarily suspended.

Tongues twittered.

"I need my beauty sleep." She paused to appreciate the polite chuckles. "And I'm not about to let the game go on unsupervised. Which brings me to my next rule—during those eight measly hours, no one is allowed to leave his or her room. Since each of your rooms has its own bath, this should not be a problem. Breakfast, incidentally, will be promptly at half past eight."

Rupert cleared his throat.

"What is it, dear?"

"What if we get hungry, Grandmother? I don't know about y'all—" he glanced at his siblings and their mates, "but I sometimes get the munchies in the middle of the night."

Mrs. Latham awarded her youngest grandchild with a fragile smile "In that case, I advise you to stock up on snacks. Anyone caught outside his or her room during restricted hours is automatically disqualified. Is that clear?"

"Yes, ma'am," we chorused.

"Good. When the lucky player finds the item in question, he or she must report to me immediately. They must not delay, even to consort with his or her partner. Is that clear?"

"Yes, ma'am." It seemed an odd rule, and one that could not possibly be enforced, but, hey, it was her game.

"Because you see," she said, eyes brighter than ever, "each player gets only one guess."

"*One* guess?" We were beginning to sound like one of the responsive readings at church.

"If someone makes a wrong guess, they are out of the game."

We even gasped in unison.

Edith, the oldest, got up the courage to speak first. "But that's so unfair, Grandmother. My Albert doesn't know the first thing about antiques. He's bound to waste his guess, which means essentially that my team only gets one."

"You could have brought in an expert," Tradd said smugly. "Then you would have three guesses."

Edith glared at her brother. "What about poor Alexandra? She doesn't even have a partner. The poor woman must be in shock."

I turned to stare at Alexandra along with the rest. She seemed both unperturbed and disgustingly beautiful to me.

"Well, dear?" her grandmother asked gently. "Are you in shock?"

Alexandra displayed her million-dollar smile. "I'm fine, Grandmother. Really, I am. It's only a game, after all, isn't it?"

Mrs. Latham smiled. "Precisely. A game, that's all it is. A game with rules and clues. And now my dears, it's time for the first clue. The item in question is somewhere on this property."

Albert raised his hand. "You mean it could be hidden in the woods?"

"Don't be tedious, dear."

Edith glanced at her husband. "She means 'yes.' The woods *is* her property."

"What about the sky?" C.J. asked.

The rest of us contestants froze.

"Well, it's possible, you know. Once, when I was a little girl, Granny Ledbetter couldn't find her dentures for almost a week. Couldn't eat anything but grits and gravy. Turns out Cousin Orville tied them to a helium balloon he got at the carnival. There they were, floating above her head the entire time."

Mrs. Latham stared at C.J. "Is that so?"

I prayed C.J. wouldn't launch into a commercial for Cousin Orville's pig teeth dentures.

C.J. returned the matriarch's stare unabashedly. "Yes, ma'am."

I breathed a sigh of relief, and somewhere in Georgetown a candle was extinguished.

Mrs. Latham actually chuckled—either that, or a bullfrog croaked beneath her chair. "Well, I'll remember your fascinating story if I ever misplace my dentures. In the meantime, are y'all ready for another clue?"

To my astonishment, Albert removed a small notebook and pen from his shirt pocket. Sally one-upped him by fishing a small tape recorder from her pocketbook.

"The item in question is in plain sight."

Heads spun. The frog croaked again.

"I didn't mean in *here*, necessarily. Although, it is quite possible—probable even, given my fondness for the room—"

"Is that another clue?" Harold whispered loudly to Sally.

"Shhh." Sally nodded in her grandmother-in-law's direction.

"As I was *about* to say," Mrs. Latham said, glaring at her grandson, "the item in question isn't hidden. Rather, it is displayed."

"Like in 'The Purloined Letter,' " C.J. burbled.

"Exactly."

C.J. turned to me triumphantly. I did my duty and poked her in the ribs. The girl was getting too big for her britches. Who knew they taught Poe in Shelby?

Rupert regarded his literate partner warily. "What's this about a pearl-lined letter?"

"Never mind," said his grandmother. "She can explain later. The final clue is a quote first attributed to John Heywood that is particularly applicable to this situation."

C.J. bounced with excitement. "Oh, you mean

the one about it not being over until the fat lady sings?"

Fortunately Mrs. Latham was too thin to be offended. "You are very amusing, dear," she said, "but your reference is to a quote by Dan Cook of the *Washington Post*. John Heywood said something quite different altogether."

C.J. turned the color of Mama's cranberry mousse. The poor girl was only trying to come off as sophisticated, but she may as well have tried initiating a game of Truth or Dare at the White House.

"It was a good try," the old lady said generously. "Now, are there any questions?"

Six hands shot up. For the record, Alexandra Latham's was not among them.

"Edith?"

"What was the quote, Grandmother?"

"Ah, but that is for me to know, and you to find out."

You should have heard the grandchildren and their spouses. The old house had not been subjected to such a litany of moans and groans since it served as a Civil War hospital.

The old lady waited patiently for several minutes. Finally she turned to me.

I stifled a gasp. "I beg your pardon, ma'am, but they"—I pointed around the room—"have been making all that noise. Not me."

She nodded. "They're all fools," she said quietly, "but what can I do?"

"You could divorce them," C.J. said.

"Oh?"

"Granny Ledbetter did that. Wrote Cousin Orville right out of her will."

The button eyes glinted with interest. "Just because he airlifted her dentures?"

"Oh, no, ma'am. It was much worse than that. It was a typical hot summer night in Shelby and he maliciously and quite purposefully unplugged her freezer."

"Causing hundreds of dollars of food to spoil," I said, trying to hurry the story along.

C.J. rolled her eyes. "Oh, Abby, don't be so silly. Granny Ledbetter didn't keep food in her freezer."

"What did she keep in it?" I asked, displaying yet again my penchant for living on the edge.

"Why, nothing. She slept in it, of course!"

There is a first time for everything, and to the best of my knowledge this was the first time I had ever seen an eighty-nine-year-old roll her eyes. I rolled mine too out of solidarity. Suddenly I was aware that the room was as quiet as church the Sunday after Easter.

"The mewling seems to have subsided," I whispered.

The grande dame smiled. "So it has. Well, children, I have one more thing to add before we adjourn to dress for dinner. But"—she turned my way—"if you two wouldn't mind, I prefer to speak to my grandchildren alone."

"Ah—" C.J.'s protest was preempted by my thumb and forefinger.

"But, Miss Cox is my partner," Rupert whined. "I don't see why you have to send *her* away." Fortunately for him, he was too far away to pinch. My children claim I am a world-class pincher, and they ought to know.

If you ask me, Mrs. Latham had more patience than a hen setting on marble eggs. She merely smiled at her youngest grandchild.

"You'll see in a minute, dear. It's a family surprise."

"I love surprises," Alexandra said softly.

Sally nudged Harold. "So do I, as long as they keep their clothes on."

Everyone laughed, perhaps too heartily. The room was full of nervous anticipation. Clearly it was time for us outsiders to exit.

I stood up. "Dmitri?" I said, taking a tentative step forward to retrieve him. He was, by then, fast asleep on the grande dame's lap.

"Leave him be, child." She caught herself. "I mean, if you don't mind. You would be doing an old lady a very big favor if you let him spend as much time with me as he wants."

That was fine with me. Peachy keen, as a matter of fact. Let the octogenarian scoop his litter box. Let her be responsible for the shredded drapes and inevitable hair balls on her bed. Let her be the recipient of mice heads and whatever other "love presents" he chose to deliver. But just wait until I got my fickle friend home—then we'd see who was in charge. Dmitri might be smart, and strong-willed, but he has yet to master a can opener. Don't get me wrong, I had no intention of starving the little beast, but I am not above withholding favorite flavors from a finicky feline.

"He's yours for the duration," I said, in a voice loud enough to wake the dead two counties over. Dmitri didn't even open his eyes.

Mrs. Elias Burton Latham III looked like she'd been handed the ten-million-dollar sweepstakes check. "I promise to take good care of him."

Without further ado C.J. and I bade a temporary farewell to the family and followed the flouncing Flora up a sweeping staircase. Call it intuition, or bad shrimp, but I had a gut feeling that something was about to go wrong with my weekend near the coast.

"Check it out!" C.J. twirled, her arms above her head. "Can you believe this place?"

"It's something else." That was, of course, an understatement. I was trying to sound cool and professional, when in reality I was lusting in my heart. Jimmy Carter would have understood, although it wasn't flesh I was lusting over, but an eighteenth-century four-poster bed with inlaid satinwood posts. Around the top of the canopy was a pierced and gilded cornice, much like a tiara, from which hung pink silk taffeta drapes.

"It's more than just something, Abby. It's awesome!"

I sighed. "There are times when I would gladly trade my firstborn for a bed like that."

"I thought you decided to forgive her, Abby."

"I have. But I could be persuaded to change my mind. Especially if you throw in that Bergamo rug you're standing on." I have a particular weakness for rugs and beds, and it has nothing to do with sexual deprivation, no matter what Greg says.

C.J. nodded. "It is a beautiful rug, but I prefer the silk Tabriz you're standing on."

I looked at my feet. "I'll throw in my secondborn as well."

"Abby, this is like the Biltmore, isn't it? Or Hearst Castle in San Simeon. I've never been to those places, but people who have, tell me that it's like dying and going to heaven."

I was afraid to ask C.J. how many dead friends she had. "Yeah, it's like those places, but they're in public hands now. All this, however, belongs to one old lady downstairs."

"Who has two unmarried grandsons. Abby, do you think Rupert likes me? I mean, he hardly said a word to me."

I shrugged. "You haven't even been alone. Just don't be surprised if Rupert is—well, you know."

"No, I don't. What do you mean?"

"Like the Rob-Bobs," I said patiently. Rob Goldburg and Bob Steuben are two dear friends of ours, fellow dealers in Charlotte, but they would no sooner be interested in C.J., than would I.

"You mean gay?"

"That's what I mean, dear. Not that there's anything wrong with being gay, of course."

"Ooh, Abby, you're just jealous because Rupert is cuter than Tradd. You want to rub your hands all over that nice, smooth head."

Rupert *cute*? I've seen boiled eggs with more attractive pates. And that cleft chin! Lord only knows what Michael Crichton might find living in a crevice that deep. I considered telling my young friend that I'd sooner eat liverwurst ice cream than rub Rupert's head. Wisely, however, I bit my tongue.

"Come on, Abby, admit it!"

"Okay, I admit it," I said. C.J. can be as relentless as a tick on a dead hound. Sometimes it pays just to give in.

C.J. beamed. "Finally, I feel like life is going my way. Of course, I owe it all to you, Abby."

"Well—"

"I always wanted to stay in a place this nice. You know, to kind of pretend it was mine. I can't wait to crawl into that four-poster tonight. Hey, Abby, which side do you want?"

"The right."

"Good, I'll take what's left." She laughed with sheer joy.

Perhaps my gut feeling was wrong. Perhaps this weekend was going to be the beginning of good things for both of us. Perhaps Calamity Jane was finally going to leave the calamity part of her behind.

"The Biltmore might be larger than this house," I said generously, "but it doesn't have a rosewood writing table as nice as that one." I pointed to a little desk with clean lines, positioned near the window. An Abby without scruples might have considered lowering it to the ground with a velvet drape after dark and having an accomplice pick it up.

C.J. grinned. "I know it's a wild fantasy, but what if I married Rupert, and his grandmother asked us to move in with her? I'd want to have this very same room."

"But you haven't even seen the other bedrooms, dear. They might—"

I may as well have been speaking to my fictional accomplice. C.J. was pirouetting around the room like an oversized ballerina, a look of rapture on her face.

"I could live in this room, and never leave!" She stopped in midturn. "Oh, look at this inlaid commode with the acanthus-leaf motif. There isn't a scratch on it. Hey, Abby, are we supposed to put our clothes in this?"

"I guess." I scanned the striped silk wallpaper. "I don't see a closet."

C.J. draped her lanky frame over a Chippendale armchair next to the commode. An *authentic* Chippendale. "Oh, man, now what am I going to do. I can't hang my gowns from the cornice, can I?"

"Do so and die," I said sweetly. Anything can happen, you know? There was an off-off chance I would marry Tradd and move into this bedroom myself. If that was the case, I didn't want any hanger marks messing up the gilded cornice.

"Abby, didn't Tradd tell you? His grandmother likes everyone to dress for dinner."

"Of course, he told me. I brought that little black dress I bought last fall, the one you can scrunch in a ball, yet it shows no wrinkles."

"Ooh, Abby, you're not serious, are you?"

"Why wouldn't I be?"

"Because in this case, dress means long skirts."

"*How* long?" The scrunchable dress stops mid-thigh. Okay, so maybe it really is a spandex blouse I wear as a dress, but you just try and buy something sexy in my size. Besides, I have great gams for a woman my age.

"*Long.* To the floor, Abby. Tradd said the women wear gowns to dinner. Didn't you bring a gown, Abby?"

I hung my head. "Not even a nightgown—but don't worry, I brought pajamas."

C.J. stroked her chin. "Well, I brought two gowns—that green one you hate so much, and a red sequined formal from the fifties that I bought at Metrolina Antique Expo. You're welcome to take your pick."

"Thanks, dear, but they're not going to fit. And I never said I hated that green gown. I just said it looks like pond algae."

C.J. got up and rummaged through an oversized bag. It was large enough to stuff a body in. Who would have thought that one girl would need so many clothes for a weekend? I, on the other hand, was traveling with one tote bag the size of a bed-room pillow.

"Hey," she said, holding up a black half slip, "there's this. If we tie it up with a belt or some-thing—under your armpits—it should just reach the floor."

"What good will that do without a gown?" I wailed.

"But *that* will be the gown, don't you see? It has plenty of lace and splits at the side. Who's to know it's not a designer gown? You don't mind showing a little shoulder, do you?"

"You're kidding, aren't you?"

She shook her head so vigorously, the stringy blond hair was a blur. "I've never been more se-rious in my life."

"Oh, God!"

"Of course, I could tell everyone that you're sick."

Thank God I had taken the time to shave that morning. And I don't mean my shoulders.

"I'm all yours," I said ruefully. "Deck me out and make me beautiful."

Trust me, it didn't look as bad it sounds. Neither of us had a belt that fit around my upper thorax—hers was too big, mine too small—but one of the velvet drape tiebacks fit the bill perfectly. So what if it was scarlet? It added a jaunty splash of color, and the tassel, which we could not remove, we managed to position directly between my bosom.

All right. So I didn't look like a million dollars. I looked like a Kmart half slip and a drapery tie-back. But my shoes were black, and if your shoes match your outfit—or so Mama says—you can get away with just about anything. Not that Mama would be caught dead with fewer than three crinolines and her ubiquitous pearls.

While I wasn't expecting a standing ovation when I swept into the salon, I was at least expecting a curious glance. But even my C.J. creation could not account for the frozen faces of the Burton-Latham clan.

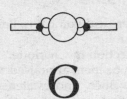

6

"Aw, come on," I wailed, "it isn't that bad."

"It's pretty awful," Tradd said, grabbing my elbow and steering me aside.

"Okay, so the tassel is a bit much, but—"

"Abby, what the hell are you talking about?"

"My dress, of course. Look, I didn't—"

"Your dress is fine."

"*What*?"

"All right, it's more than fine. You're a knockout in it."

I let that percolate for a minute. "Then what's so awful?"

"Grandmother's little surprise, that's what."

"Which is?"

"Sorry, sworn to secrecy. Hey, you want something to drink?"

"Got a Bailey's?" Okay, so maybe Irish cream whiskey is more of an after-dinner drink, than a cocktail, but it is a favorite of mine, and what was there to lose? How any more déclassé can one get than to wear a friend's half slip to dinner?

The second Tradd left to get my drink, Sally floated over in a peach chiffon number. "Love your dress, dear. Where did you get it, Bergdorf's in Atlanta?"

"The Cox collection in Charlotte."

The blue-gray peepers appraised me again. "It's really exquisite. Such understatement in design. Perhaps I saw one like it on a runway in Milan. It looks somehow familiar, you know?"

"Does it?" I twisted my torso just enough to set the tassel in motion. "Well, I assure you, it's one of a kind. Cox is a personal friend, and made the gown just for me."

She nodded. "I hope you won't be offended, dear, but I must have one just like it for the Art Guild dinner next month. Do you suppose that's possible?"

"I guarantee it. Say, why was everybody looking so grim when I walked in?"

Tradd's arm shot through the space between Sally and me, and the Bailey's materialized under my nose.

"I got it on the rocks," he said. "You didn't specify."

"Rocks are preferred. Thanks." I glanced around, but Sally had slipped behind me and was engaged in conversation with C.J. If ever my pal were to come down with a case of lockjaw, would that it be then. I mean, considering all the times she'd stuck her foot in her mouth, she was bound to have scratched her gums on a rusty grommet at least once.

I took a step backward, the better to eavesdrop, when an obnoxious-sounding gong sounded inches from my ear. I whirled.

"Dinner," Flora mouthed. At least that's what I think she said. The gong noise was still reverberating in my ear.

Tradd grabbed my elbow again. "Let the others go first."

Flora shot me a look capable of piercing a rhino's hide, wheeled, and marched from the room. The others departed without drama.

"So, Abby," Tradd said, when we were alone, "did you see anything?"

"Besides a faux-French maid who has the hots for you?"

"Not that. Flora's old news. I mean in your room."

I blinked. "I saw lots of things in my room. Beautiful things. And they're all still there."

"You sure?"

"Of course!" I fully intended to return the tassel, so it was only a lie from a technical point of view.

"But how can you be so sure?"

"Well, uh—I don't know what you mean."

"Like she has all the bedrooms crammed with things. You know, beds, dressers, whatever. How would you know if something was missing? By the difference in wallpaper shades?"

"Could be. Or from marks in carpets, or dents in floors. But if it's a small item, something that sits on a dresser top or commode, well—then there wouldn't be any way to tell."

"It doesn't make any sense, you know? Something that's missing, but still in plain sight."

I sipped my cream whiskey. "It could be as simple as something out of place. Something out of order. Which means it could be anything."

He squinted at a painting across the room. "Well, not *anything*. It has to be something you can hide something in."

"Why is that?"

"Uh—"

A snort from the doorway announced Flora's presence. "Mrs. Latham said to come. Y'all are holding things up."

Tradd all but jumped for the door. I scurried after him, holding my slip aloft so that I wouldn't trip.

"Slut," Flora whispered as I brushed past.

"Tramp," I murmured behind me.

"Whore."

I stopped and turned. That was going too far.

"Listen here, you—"

"Abby!" Tradd called from down the hall.

I waggled a threatening finger at Flora. "I'll tell Mrs. Latham."

Flora shrugged insolently. "Nice slip," she said, and ducked into the salon.

Everyone was seated when we arrived. I have never been so embarrassed in my life. Even the time Mama showed up at a Charlotte reception for an English countess, with Stan, her muscle-bound houseboy, paled in comparison. All eyes were on us, Mrs. Latham's in particular, which glittered like black plastic buttons from across the room.

"Sorry, ma'am," Tradd said. "Abby had to use the powder room."

I could feel myself flush. "And a beautiful room it is too, ma'am."

"Sit," she said, nodding at the two open places.

She sat at the head of the table, and unfortunately both vacancies were on either side of her. I sat down obediently, next to Edith Burton Jansen. From the look of things, our hostess didn't follow the old boy-girl-boy rule. And instead of a male at the foot of the table, there sat C.J., resplendent in her slime-green dress.

The old biddy smiled thinly. "Well, now that we're all here, let's say grace. Edith, dear, do you mind?"

Edith immediately launched into the longest extemporaneous prayer these Episcopalian ears have ever heard. We Frozen Chosen tend to stick to prayers found in the Book of Common Prayer, but Edith seemed to gather her inspiration from everywhere. I wouldn't have been surprised to hear the Kama Sutra referenced. Finally, after a verbal meandering through world literature, Edith settled down and blessed the food for ten minutes.

There followed a chorus of amens, and a few genuine sighs of relief.

"I thought y'all were Episcopalians," I said casually, when the sighs subsided.

"We are," Mrs. Latham said, the pride evident in her voice. "Edith's prayer is an old family prayer. We add to it with each generation. Each member gets to add a line when they turn eighteen. Isn't it wonderful?"

"It's awesome."

"I used to be able to recite all of it, but I can't keep up anymore. We've had so many birthdays lately."

"Our son just turned eighteen," Albert said proudly. "He added the line about the doughnuts."

"You don't say." I am a doughnut addict, and was about to suggest that the next natal celebrant eliminate everything *except* the doughnut clause, when Flora appeared once more, bearing a tray of salads.

She served Mrs. Latham first. "Cook's gone home," she whispered as she set down a bowl.

"What?"

"Cook's gone home," Flora said louder.

"Speak up, child. You know my hearing's not what it used to be."

"The damn cook's gone home," Flora shouted.

"But why?"

"Cut her finger slicing tomatoes, ma'am. But don't worry, I rinsed them off."

"I think I'm going to be sick," Edith moaned.

"Cook *was*," Flora said dryly. "That's why there's no soup."

Rupert leaned forward and raised his hand. "Grandmother, can we skip to the main course?"

Flora snickered, but said nothing.

"Speak up, child," her mistress snapped.

"Uh-well, ma'am—uh, I was helping cook, taking the roast out of the oven when she screamed. I guess I kind of dropped it."

"You guess?"

"Okay, I dropped it. But it's all right now. I picked most the glass off. I even rinsed it under water. Only it's not as brown as it was."

Edith moaned again.

I rolled my eyes behind closed lids.

Mrs. Latham put her napkin back on the table. "Well, I guess we have no option then but to send someone in to Georgetown for takeout. Any volunteers?"

Beautiful, reserved Alexandra cleared her throat before speaking. No doubt she needed to clear the cobwebs out that accumulated between usage.

"Grandmother, if you don't mind, I'd like to try my hand in the kitchen. I saw some eggs and a little cold chicken in the refrigerator earlier. And I think a jar of artichokes. I could make some omelettes if you like."

Our hostess beamed. "Bless you, child. I always disliked those burger things. Combos, jumbos, juniors—it doesn't make sense. But an omelette now, that would be lovely. And Flora here can help you."

Flora scowled. "I ain't paid to do no cooking," she muttered. "Clean the house, that's it."

"Oh, stop it now, and hurry along. You're more capable than you think. You did just fine serving the punch and canapés yesterday."

"Yes, ma'am, but like I told you, I dropped the roast."

"Flora!"

The maid muttered something unintelligible. Much to my disappointment the old lady did not ask her to repeat it, neither did she respond. She just stared at Flora with those bright black eyes, and after a few seconds Flora wilted.

It was such a letdown to see Flora trot out of the room docilely on the heels of elegant Alexandra. Not that I liked Flora, mind you, or disliked Mrs. Latham. It's just that I've always found that a good argument—as long as I'm not personally involved—stimulates the appetite.

"Grandmother, you might consider firing her," Edith said, her eyes fixed straight ahead.

"Fire her? Whatever for?"

"She's impertinent, Grandmother."

"Is that it?"

"And she steals," Sally said.

"I don't need your help," Edith growled, her lips barely moving.

Mrs. Latham ignored her eldest grandchild, if indeed she'd heard her. "*Steals*?"

"Yes, ma'am. I wasn't going to tell you this, but last summer I saw Flora slip something in her handbag. Something from your desk in the study.

When she saw me, she looked like she'd seen a ghost."

The corners of Mrs. Latham's mouth turned slightly upwards, like the edges of a crépe. "And what were you doing in my study, dear?"

Sally colored. "I was looking for you."

"I see. Let's hope you found me. So, what did Flora put in her handbag?"

Sally shrugged, her color deepening. "I wasn't close enough to see, ma'am. But she looked guilty."

The crépe collapsed. "That's hardly a reason to fire her. With the exception of our two guests from Charlotte, each and every one of you looks guilty to me."

"That's preposterous," Albert said, his tone rising and then falling, as he lost his nerve. "We have absolutely no reason to feel guilty, do we, dear?"

Edith nodded. She had forsaken the diamond posts in favor of diamond drops. The latter swung seductively, and I longed to snatch them from her brown lobes.

"Well, I do," Harold said.

All eyes turned his way.

"I stole some of your shampoo, Grandmother."

"You stole it?"

"Well, I used it without your permission. You see, I ran out of shampoo the last time I was here— and Sally's stinks to high heaven—so I took yours. Only it turns out it wasn't shampoo after all, but bath oil. Even though I rinsed as well as I could, that night my head kept slipping off the pillow."

Everyone laughed, including the grande dame.

"Dear, dear, Harold," she said.

"Dumb, dumb, Harold," Edith grunted.

"Laugh," C.J. said somberly, "but I had an aunt

in Shelby who did something like that, only it turned out awful."

Mrs. Latham smiled benevolently down the length of the table. "What happened to your aunt, dear?"

"Auntie Agnes accidentally brushed her teeth with hemorrhoid cream. Her mouth puckered up like a dried fig and she couldn't talk for a week."

I'm ashamed to say that I prayed C.J. would make the same mistake, and the sooner the better. To my dismay everyone howled at C.J.'s account, including hard-hearted Edith.

"You're a hoot, you know that?" Rupert blew his weekend date a kiss. He looked a lot more normal now that he was wearing a dark suit and tie. If he lost the earring, grew hair, and spackled in his chin, he might even be good-looking. Almost as handsome as Tradd.

"But it wasn't funny," C.J. protested. She looked embarrassedly away from the group. Her gaze scanned the walls for a few seconds. Then her mouth popped open. It was as if her bottom jaw had become unhinged. She made a few choking sounds.

Tradd, who was sitting next to her on the left, patted her gently on the back. "Hey, you all right?"

She gasped a few times. "Fine as frog's hair. But I need to speak to Mrs. Latham."

The grande dame had been watching C.J.'s drama with interest. This I could tell by the tightening lines around her mouth. Bird eyes told me nothing.

"What is it, dear?" the old woman asked.

"I need to speak to you alone."

"Can it wait until after supper, dear? We could have coffee together in the salon. Perhaps you'll share some more of your delightful Shelby stories."

"I need to speak to you now."

"Well—"

"*Now.*"

"Really, dear—"

"It has to be now."

"Stop it, C.J.," I hissed. "Mind your manners!"

C.J. threw her hands up in the air. "All right, but I was just trying to follow the rules. She said to tell her the second we knew what the missing item is, and to do it in private."

"So?" I snapped.

"So, I know what it is," C.J. crowed.

You could have heard darkness fall in that room.

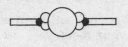

7

Mrs. Latham stood slowly, with almost exaggerated care. She was eighty-nine, after all, just eleven years away from meeting official government standards for antiques.

"Come with me, child," she said.

C.J. bounced to her feet. "Yes, ma'am!"

Rupert stood as well. "Grandmother?"

"Yes, Rupert?"

"May I come too?"

"Have you a guess to make?"

"No, ma'am, but Miss Cox is my partner."

"Sit down, Rupert."

"But Grandmother!"

The grande dame closed her eyes, and I knew from my own experience as a mother, that she was praying for patience. "Sit, child."

"Please, Grandmother. *Please*. Pretty please."

Dmitri whines like that when I won't let him go outside. I invariably give in, but I'm a pushover for fur balls with retractable claws. Perhaps if Rupert didn't shave his head, he would have better luck.

"Rupert William Alexander Latham Burton!" Mrs. Latham spat his names out as if they were cotton balls. "You will sit down and be quiet, or you will go to your room."

Rupert wilted into his seat.

"Good. Now, if y'all will be so kind as to excuse us"—she motioned to C.J.—"I would like to speak to this young lady alone."

C.J. can be a dear when she wants to, and she strode around the table and gallantly offered the old lady her arm. The rest of us sat, still as mummies, until the dining room door closed behind them. Then they pounced on me.

Edith grabbed my arm. "What did she see?"

I pried her loose. "How should I know?"

Albert leaned across the table. "Is this Miss Cox really an expert?"

"She's good, but she's not the best." Hey, I was only being honest.

"Abby's the best," Tradd said,

"She's not a distant cousin, is she? Look how she's sucking up to the old bag!"

"Rupert!" Harold roared. "Just shut up."

"That's telling him," I said.

Harold rewarded me with a smirk. "He was wasting time. Now answer my sister's question. What did Ms. Cox see?"

"She saw a band of angels coming after me," I crooned.

"What the—are you nuts?"

"You're not even on my team, dear. We shouldn't be talking about this."

Harold turned to his brother. "I thought you said she was the best. Hell, she's just loony tunes."

I pushed back my chair and stood up—one needs to expand one's diaphragm fully for maximum volume—and belted out the refrain from one of my favorite spirituals. "Swing low, sweet chariot, coming for to carry me home! Swing low, sweet chariot. Coming for to carry me home."

All right, so I don't possess the best set of pipes in the world, but neither do I sound like a long-tailed cat on a porch full of rockers—like Mama. There is a rumor going around church that she pays the choir director for the privilege of making her joyful noise unto the Lord. I'm pretty sure that rumor is false. But about the rumor that she slept with him—Mama made that one up herself.

"Brava! Brava!"

I spun around. The grande dame was actually applauding. If pressed, I will confess that this was a new experience for me. At any rate, I decided to run with it.

"I can do 'Memories,' " I said. "Would you like to hear a few stanzas?"

"Some other time, dear."

"I'm still working on 'Don't Cry For Me, Argentina,' but—"

"Abby!" Tradd said, with surprising sharpness.

I hushed my mouth. I can take a hint. Besides, I had just noticed that our hostess was standing in the doorway by herself. The real fruitcake was nowhere to be seen. The others noticed her absence as well.

"Where is she?" Edith practically screamed.

"Was she right?" Harold hollered.

Albert snorted. "Of course, she was right, that's why she's upstairs right now packing her bags. She's about to make off with your grandmother's loot."

"So much for teamwork," Rupert moaned.

Mrs. Latham calmly took her seat, smoothed her napkin in her lap, and smiled beneficently. "Every now and then I have the privilege of meeting an exceptional individual, one who delights my soul. Well, children, this Jane Cox—this C.J.—is just such a person."

"But she's an outsider and an impostor," Sally hissed. "Mrs. Timberlake admitted that while you were gone."

"I did not! I merely said that she wasn't as much of an expert as I. Besides, I wasn't the one who said it. Tradd was."

"*Really?*" Mrs. Latham turned to her middle grandson. "Is that so?"

The sun began to set in Tradd's golden eyes. "Uh, well, I—"

"Never mind, dear. I'm eighty-nine, remember? I don't have that much time left. Anyway, it doesn't matter. The girl guessed wrong, so she's out of the game."

Rupert moaned again. "Ah, man, this bites."

"I *beg* your pardon?"

"Nothing."

"Nothing what?"

"Nothing, *ma'am.*" It was the correct word, but an incorrect response nonetheless.

"Say it again, Rupert." Frostier words have seldom been spoken this far south.

"Geez, Grandmother. I don't know what the big deal is. You're always carrying on like it's the beginning of World War III. No wonder Mama ran away from home so many times."

Our collective gasps extinguished one of the candles in the centerpiece.

Fortunately for Rupert's hide the door to the kitchen swung open to reveal the ravishing Alexandra bearing a tray of omelettes.

*   *   *

Thank goodness the woman was only a fair cook. Otherwise I might have had to hate her along with the others. It was difficult enough to take the middle road, and just envy her. Looks, money, height—if I had that woman's gifts, I could have my choice of men. And many women. Not that the latter is an interest of mine, but a fact is a fact.

We ate our so-so omelettes in relative silence. Please pass the salt, please pass the pepper, a few murmured thank-yous, that was the extent of our conversation. Mrs. Latham, of course, complimented Alexandra's cooking skills with every bite, but I'm not counting that. My point is, we may as well have been pigs lined up at a trough, thanks to Rupert's penchant for getting his grandmother's goat. What a waste of food.

I, for one, was dying to know what had become of C.J. But, I am ashamed to say, I lacked the nerve to inquire. A mediocre meal is better than none, and I was afraid of being sent to my room. I made a mental note to stuff myself and my purse with the shrimp canapés before supper, should history repeat itself.

"Oh, my." Mrs. Latham sighed pointedly at the meal's conclusion. "Cook and Flora usually do the clearing together. But look at all this mess—and poor Flora, all by herself now that cook is gone."

"Don't worry, Grandmother, I'll help." Alexandra was back on her feet, brimming with do-gooder energy.

Even I wanted to retch. At least I didn't make soft, but disgusting sounds like the others. And to think they were adults!

The matriarch, however, seemed oblivious to granddaughter's manipulative ways. "What a good girl you are, Andie. Just like your father in so many ways. My little Eddie was always such a considerate boy.

This was too much even for the fair Alexandra. "Grandmother, please."

"But it's true. Did you know that once when your father was a little boy—three years old, to be exact—he gave his entire allowance to a beggar?"

"Yes, ma'am." At least Alexandra had the decency to blush, but it was not a shade becoming a natural redhead.

"He made me so proud that day. Imagine, a little tyke like that, filled with the spirit of generosity. Just marched up to that beggar in Charleston and handed him that fifty-cent piece."

"I thought that happened in Georgetown," Edith said boldly. Supper was over, after all, there was nothing to lose.

"We don't have beggars in Georgetown," Mrs. Latham said crisply. She stood up. "Well, children, I wish I could say that the weekend has been a pleasure so far, but, it hasn't. Perhaps tomorrow things will be different."

She made her way regally to the door, then stopped, and turned slowly. "I'm more tired than anticipated, so I shall be retiring now. Have fun with your game, but don't forget the most important rule. Anyone caught outside his or her room between the hours of midnight and eight is automatically disqualified." She paused for dramatic effect. "Is that clear?"

"Yes, ma'am," we bleated in unison.

Edith was on her feet the second the grande dame's derriere cleared the door. "Well, whatever it is, it's not in this room," she declared.

Howard stood slowly. "What makes you so sure?"

Edith rested brown hands on beige hips. They were the first beige sequins I had ever seen. No doubt the woman worked hard to be so bland.

"It's just like Clue," she said. She was speaking in what I will charitably call her "big-sister voice." "Miss Cox guessed Professor Plum with the leaf pipe in the dining room. Well, she was wrong, wasn't she? So we know it's not the dining room."

Sally shook her head vigorously. "But we don't know that, at all. It could still be the dining room, but with Miss Scarlet and the candelabra."

"Y'all aren't making a lick of sense," Rupert whined.

"Clue is a board game," I explained kindly. "Not that it matters. Those rules don't apply here, anyway. But if they did, Professor Plum would be your grandmother. We already know *who* hid the item in question, we just don't know what the item is, or its location."

Alexandra yawned. "Except that it has something to do with the river."

"*What*?" The question was on everyone's lips, including mine.

"When I was in the kitchen making the omelettes I remembered the John Heywood quote, or a variation thereof. It came to me just like that, thanks to something Flora said. Not that what Flora said had anything to do with John Heywood. You know, it's funny how things will pop into one's head at the oddest times. I mean, there I am cracking eggs while Flora's slicing artichoke hearts—"

"What's the quote?" we screamed.

Alexandra yawned again. " 'Time and tide wait

for no man.' You can find it in any comprehensive book of quotes."

"The boathouse!" Edith barked.

I'm sure she meant to bark only at Albert, but we all heard it. The stampede that ensued was worthy of a buffalo herd. When the dust cleared only Alexandra and I remained.

"You don't seem to take this game very seriously," I said

"Oh, but I am. As soon as the quote came to me I ran out to the boathouse. But you see, there's nothing there. Just a leaky old boat in a rickety old building with a sagging dock. And a stupid old chest filled with lifesavers. Oh, and cobwebs. Plenty of those."

"Ah, so that's why the omelettes took so long! You were playing sleuth while we waited for our supper."

Alexandra allowed a smile to part the perfect lips. "Well, that, and the fact that Flora is all thumbs when it comes to cooking. Didn't you think that the omelettes tasted a little strange?"

"Well, now that you mention it, I did."

"That's because while I was off checking the boathouse, Flora—"

"I don't *even* want to hear it," I said, and went off in search of C.J.

I found my young friend lying face down, sobbing, on that magnificent eighteenth-century four-poster bed.

"C.J.! What is it?"

She sat up, and I tried not to gasp. Greg claims that there are a few women—he says I'm one of them—who actually look better after crying. I think he means this as a compliment. Apparently C.J. is not of this select group. She looked like a strawberry cream pie that had collided with a hot waffle iron.

"Oh, Abby, I want to go home!"

"There, there," I said, and made a concerted effort to gather her gangly frame in my arms and give her a maternal hug.

C.J. pushed me away. "Abby, please! I'm embarrassed enough."

I sat on the bed beside her, doing my best to ignore the bright pink blotches on the silk bedspread that were C.J.'s tears. What if they dried as stains, or left puckers? Thanks to the discovery of DNA, at least the grande dame couldn't pin the ruined spread on me.

"There is no reason on earth to be embarrassed, C.J."

"Yes, there is; I made a fool of myself! And I shouldn't have guessed first."

"Someone had to guess first. Personally, I think it was very brave of you."

"You do?"

"Absolutely."

"But I bet they're all laughing at me."

I handed her a clump of tissues. Thanks to Mama's tutelage I never travel anywhere without a pound or two of paper products.

C.J. blew her nose loudly. "*Are* they?"

I pictured the thundering herd stampeding into the empty boathouse. "No, they're not laughing."

"I just know that Rupert will never speak to me again."

"Consider yourself fortunate, dear. The man is a whining loser."

She honked again. "Abby, that's easy for you to say. Men are always falling over you."

"I can't help it if I'm short. They should look where they're going."

She giggled. "No, I'm serious. Look at Greg. Tall, dark and handsome—and he'd give his eye teeth to get you back."

"And I'd be happy to help him pull them."

"Ooh, Abby, you're bad. But you always know how to make me feel better. You know that?"

I shrugged, feeling guilty. The girl is one of my peripheral friends, after all. Her name is not likely to appear on my social calendar unless my other friends—the A list—are all busy.

"Are you hungry, dear?" I asked. It wouldn't hurt me to go down to the kitchen and scrounge up something for her to eat. I'm not the world's best cook, but even I could compete with Alexandra.

"Nah, I've got stuff right here. But thanks, anyway."

"What kind of *stuff*?"

"Candy bars. Three Musketeers."

"You wouldn't have one to spare, would you?"

C.J. rummaged in her suitcase and produced a freezer bag containing eight candy bars. "Hey, Abby, you want to watch a little TV?"

"I haven't seen a set since we arrived, dear. I don't think the boob tube is part of the Burton-Latham world."

"Yeah, but I kinda figured that would be the case, so I brought my own."

"You didn't!"

C.J. trotted back to her magic suitcase. I was beginning to think that battered old valise was capable of producing all sorts of wonders, just like David Copperfield's pants. Or Greg's pants, to hear him brag.

It was a small set, but C.J. had had the foresight to bring along an antenna. So, when I should have been downstairs trying to earn a buck, or at the least keeping an eye on things, I found myself ensconced on a vintage bed, with a B-list buddy, watching B-grade movies.

Take it from me; a gal can get herself into a lot of trouble that way.

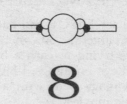

8

The last thing I remember was Doris Day slapping Rock Hudson. Or was that Sophia Loren slapping Cary Grant? Surely it wasn't Curly slapping Moe. At any rate, despite the sugar and caffeine contained in those chocolate bars, I fell asleep close to midnight, and slept straight through until eight forty-five the next morning. I was still wearing my "designer" gown when I nodded off, because I was half expecting Tradd, or even Rupert, to knock on the door, and beg our participation in the goings-on.

But they didn't. When I woke up sunlight was streaming in between the velvet drapes, and C.J. was snoring away beside me. I was astounded. It was the first time that I can recall ever having slept through an entire night without having to heed the call of nature. And the fact that I managed sleep through C.J.'s snores was nothing short of miraculous. The woman has a vibrating uvula that can wake the dead as far away as Utah.

"C.J.!"

Snrrrrrrx

I shook her, gently at first, and then made like the paint mixer at Home Depot.

"Go away!"

"C.J., it's me, Abby. Curfew is over, and if we don't shake a leg, breakfast will be, too."

"A shake for breakfast sounds good."

I whacked her with my pillow. "Up, up!"

She sat up slowly, like an aging sea monster rising from a sea of silk. "Aagh! It's so bright out."

"It's called morning, dear."

"Oh, Abby, close the curtains. All that light is giving me a pounding headache."

As if on cue someone outside our door rapped sharply.

"We'll be right there," I called brightly.

"You see," C.J. wailed, "even you can hear it!"

"It's the door, dear. Be a doll, and answer it, will you? I forgot to pack a robe."

C.J. groaned. "Do I have to? My head's killing me. Besides, you're wearing the same thing now you wore last night. They've seen it all before."

"That's precisely why I *can't* answer the door, dear. They'll think I slept in my clothes."

"But you did sleep in your clothes."

"Actually, I slept in your clothes and a drapery tieback. Now answer the door."

Our visitor, lacking the patience of Job, began pounding in earnest. It's a good thing they used solid doors back in the days of Col. Elias Latham. A hollow, particle-board door would have given way under the onslaught of fists.

"Open up in there," a male voice shouted. It sounded like Harold Burton. "Open up, or I'll have to break down the door."

I snatched the silk spread, flung a corner over either shoulder, and staggered for the door. Someone was going to get a piece of my mind.

"You tell 'em, Abby," C.J. called encouragingly from the safe comfort of the bed.

"Hold your horses!" I shouted and flung open the door.

Sure enough, it was Harold Burton, his fist raised in midblow. It was a small comfort that Harold, surprised by the sudden absence of a hard surface on which to bring down his fist, lost his balance and plunged headlong into the room. Thanks to all the karate classes Mama dragged me to, I was able to step adroitly aside.

I graciously helped the groaning man to his feet. "Most folks are more civilized when they call their guests to breakfast. A few folks even serve their guests in bed."

Harold gingerly touched his chin, which seemed to have taken the brunt of his fall. "You can forget about having breakfast."

"But we're only fifteen minutes late, dear. And it doesn't have to be fancy. Cold cereal will do just fine, won't it, C.J.?"

"Ooh, I just love cold cereal! Do y'all have Chocolate Cheeseburger Crunch?"

"There isn't going to be any damned breakfast!" Harold roared. "There's been a murder."

"*What*?"

"Don't you ladies play dumb with me. Flora is dead, and one of you killed her. Now come with me."

To his credit Harold permitted me to slip on a pair of stone-washed jeans and a brand-new T-shirt from the Gap. I know, those might sound a little casual for a weekend jaunt to the fabled Burton-Latham estate, but we're living in a new, less-structured age now where just about anything goes. Besides, they were both clean.

The rest of the clan had already assembled in the drawing room, and they stared at us as we filed in. Even the grande dame was there, although she seemed to have replaced her flat button eyes with a pair of laser beams. I could feel those babies bore into me like a pastry funnel into a cream cake.

"I told you she was trash," Edith said to Tradd.

"I am not!" I said hotly. "I come from an old, well-respected family. My great-great-granddaddy was a major in the War between the States. He sold both his mules to buy clothes for his troops."

"*Poor* white trash."

"Wow, isn't that something," C.J. exclaimed, her eyes wide with wonder. "My great-great-*great*-granddaddy was a major, too. Only he sold out his troops to buy clothes for his mules."

"No wonder the South lost the war," I moaned. I turned to Tradd. "What's this about Flora being murdered. Surely you don't believe that either C.J. or I had anything to do with it?"

The golden orbs flickered. "Of course not. But Flora was found dead in her room this morning. She'd been stabbed in the chest."

I shuddered. Death by burning would be my last choice. Death by a blade—of any description—runs a close second.

"When did it happen?"

Tradd shrugged.

"As if you don't know," Sally sneered.

"Well, I don't! I went to my room right after supper, and didn't leave until Harold came up and got us."

"And I'm her witness," C.J. said loyally. "Not that Abby needs one, of course. She can't even open a jar of peanut butter without help, much less stab anyone to death. Besides, Abby's so short, she couldn't possibly have stabbed Flora in the chest; the knife would have hit Flora in the knees."

"This is no time to be funny, dear," I said through gritted teeth.

Albert clapped his hands. "Did you hear that, folks? She said 'knife!' "

I glared at him. "So?"

"So, who said it was a knife? It could have been an ice pick, or a screwdriver."

"Or a *kris*," C.J. said.

"A *what*?" Mrs. Latham spoke in a voice so thin and sharp it could have sliced bread.

C.J., startled, took a step backward, tripped on her own feet, and nearly fell to the floor. It took a moment for her to recover.

"A kris is a kind of knife, ma'am," I said on C.J.'s behalf.

"I know what a kris is," the grande dame said crisply. "The Sultan of Bandar gave that kris to my husband and me when we toured his country on our honeymoon."

"What kris?" I glanced around the room. "Where?"

"The one in poor Flora's chest," Edith hissed.

I pointedly wiped her spittle from my face. "I didn't even know your grandmother owned a kris." I turned to Tradd. "Did you?"

"No." Okay, so he wasn't a knight in shining armor, but he didn't seem as anxious to draw and quarter me as did the others.

"I kept the kris in my room," Mrs. Latham said. She was back to button eyes. Even her voice had gone flat. "Did I ever tell you that the sultan wanted me for his harem?"

"No, grandmother," Tradd said politely.

"Well, he did. He offered your grandfather a bag of uncut rubies and a purebred Arabian stallion."

"What a coincidence," C.J. managed to say before I clamped a hand over her mouth.

"Omar was his name. The sultan's, not the horse. He was a very handsome man. But even if I didn't love your grandfather—well, the sultan already had eight wives, and who knows how many concubines. Still, it was a great honor just to be asked. There were times, in the years to come, that I almost wished we'd taken him up on his offer. Your grandfather, as you may recall, was not the kindest of men. And he might have had only one wife, but—"

Edith laid a brown arm around the grande dame's left shoulder. "Grandmother, *please*, must we share family secrets with *them*?"

Alexandra, who had been sitting very still, alabaster hands folded in lap, jumped to her feet and embraced her grandmother's right shoulder. "Well, I think it's a beautiful, romantic story. What almost was—the road not taken—lost loves, you know. I see it as a movie. Maybe with Tori Spelling playing you and—"

"Suck up," somebody hissed.

"I could play Grandfather," Rupert said. He sounded serious. "I already live in L.A., and I took an acting class last year."

Edith glared at her youngest brother. "Well, as long as we're casting the movie, I suggest we get Miss Cox here to play dead Flora."

"Ooh," C.J. said, "I could do that. I was in the drama club in high school, and Flora and I were about the same height."

"She was being facetious," I whispered. "She didn't really mean that."

Edith had ears like a bat. "Don't you tell me what I mean, or don't mean. And speaking of your friend here, she *is* the same size as poor dead Flora. Maybe you couldn't have overpowered Flora and killed her with Grandmother's fancy knife, but Miss Cox is another story."

The doorbell rang, and C.J. and I both nearly jumped out of our skins.

"Oh, didn't I tell you?" Harold said smugly. "I called the sheriff before I went up and got you. That should be him now."

"One of you is going to pay," someone said softly.

I stared at beautiful Alexandra. In her large, blue-gray eyes was a look of pure hate.

Sheriff Neely Thompson did not fit the stereotype of a southern lawman; he was black, his stomach was taut, rippling with muscles—or so I imagined—and he did not have a cigar hanging out of his mouth. He was perhaps in his late forties, of average height, with a full head of hair, worn natural. Alas, the thick gold ring on his left hand made it eminently clear he was married.

"Good morning," the sheriff said, nodding to each of us in turn, before giving his full attention to Mrs. Latham. "Good morning, Genevieve."

My heart sank. The fact that he was on a first-name basis with the grande dame meant they were old friends. There wasn't even a "Miss" thrown in there as a sign of deference.

"Good morning, Neely. How are the fish biting up your way?"

"Not so good—it's been too hot lately on the

river. But I bought a new outboard for my big boat and when the grouper start moving this fall, I'm taking her out on the ocean."

"I caught a sixty-pound marlin the year I got married," the old lady said wistfully. "Elias caught nothing. We almost called the wedding off."

Sheriff Thompson laughed. "Lucky for me, Denise hates to fish. But she likes being out on the water. Always brings a book or two."

"How is Denise? Will she be teaching again this fall?"

"Man, oh, man," C.J. moaned, tapping her foot dangerously.

Sheriff Thompson foolishly ignored her. "Guess you haven't heard yet. She's decided to go back to Clemson for her Ph.D. I'm afraid that when the grouper run, I'll be fishing by myself. Unless, of course, you care to go with me."

The grande dame chuckled. "Careful, Neely. I might just take you up on that."

"Don't think I'm kidding. I got a new reel for Christmas that purrs like a kitten. You're welcome to give it a try."

"Arrrrrgh!" C.J. wailed.

We all stared at the spectacle from Shelby. Her hands were pressed tightly against her head, as if to hold it together in the event of an explosion. From the looks of her bulging eyes, the disaster was imminent.

"You have to excuse her," I said. "She hasn't had her breakfast, and all this talk of fishing has made her hungry."

Mrs. Latham recoiled in indignation. "Breakfast! At a time like this?"

"Arrrrrgh," C.J. wailed again.

I did the loving thing and slapped my young

protégé. It was a gentle slap, mind you, and I took care to hit neither eye nor ear. Trust me, under the circumstances, it was the right thing to do.

At last the girl found her tongue. "*Please*," she begged the sheriff, "if you're going to arrest me, do it now and get it over with!"

"*Arrest* you?"

Letting go of her head, C.J. thrust both hands out. "Here. Cuff me, but be careful of the mole on my left wrist. If it gets irritated it might turn into cancer."

Sheriff Thompson smiled. "Maybe it is time I got down to business. Okay, if that's the way you want it, Miss—"

"I knew it! I knew you were onto me." She turned. "Goodbye, Abby."

"C.J.—"

"My keys are in the zippered pouch in my purse. Please, Abby, water my plants at home. And feed Cicero."

"Cicero?"

"I bought an iguana last month for my birthday. Didn't I tell you? And you thought I was still living alone."

Reptiles give me the heebie-jeebies. Perhaps it is because I was married to one for twenty years.

"Well—uh—"

"He's very tame, Abby. He'll eat lettuce right from your lips."

"I don't even think so."

"Take what you want from my shop as payment." She turned back to Sheriff Thompson. "Will they be vertical or horizontal stripes?"

"I beg your pardon, ma'am?"

"I'm kind of tall, you see, and vertical stripes might be too much. But I have broad shoulders and sort of a big bottom, so horizontal is out. Would it be possible to compromise and go for diagonal?"

Sheriff Thompson bit his lip. His eyes were dancing.

"We don't use stripes in my jail. We use polka dots. You get your choice of large or small."

C.J. breathed a sigh of relief. "I always did look good in polka dots—large, of course. They make me look smaller. Do I get to choose blue?"

Sheriff Thompson nodded. "Any other requests?"

C.J. shook her head. "So, do I confess here, or at the station?"

I grabbed one of her outstretched hands. "Don't be ridiculous, C.J. All this nonsense could land you in a heap of trouble."

She shook loose. "But I'm already in a heap of trouble, don't you see? I killed Flora."

9

I felt faint, just like the night Buford announced he was trading me in for Tweetie, who was less than half my age. It happened a week before our twentieth wedding anniversary, and I can remember it like it happened yesterday. We were getting ready for bed, and in a rare moment of boldness, I put the moves on my own husband.

"Not now," he said, surprisingly gruff.

"What's the matter?" I teased. "Have a headache?"

He colored, something I mistook then as a coy blush.

I giggled. "Maybe if I give you a massage, your headache will go away."

"It isn't a headache, Abby. We're through."

"I know you're usually too quick, dear, but this time we haven't even begun!"

"I'm not joking, Abby. You know that new secretary the firm hired?"

"You mean Silicone Valley?"

"Yeah, that's the one, but her name is Tweetie Moreno."

"You mean Tweetie like the bird?"

"Stop it, Abby. I'm trying to tell you it's over between us. I want a divorce."

That's when I felt faint. My head spun, my vision blurred, and it was as if someone had punched me in the soft spots behind both knees. I sat heavily down on our turned-back bed.

"What has she got that I don't?" I wailed.

As if it wasn't obvious. Two decades of marriage down the drain because of two handfuls of petroleum derivatives. How shallow can someone get?

"See her bust size, and raise her two," I said.

What was I talking about? Although there were any number of plastic surgeons in Charlotte who would be happy to sell me a chest, with my small frame I couldn't achieve even Tweetie's dimensions without toppling over.

"Aw, get it off, Abby. It isn't just her boobs. It's who she is. Tweetie makes me feel like a young man again."

"And what do I make you feel like?" I shouted. "Chopped liver?"

Okay, so I was getting carried away by one of my most miserable memories, but that didn't warrant a slap from C.J.

"Abby!"

I reeled, more from shock than the impact. Face it, C.J. might be a big gal, but she has poor follow-through. Apparently she is also very fond of me.

"Ooh, Abby, I'm so sorry! It's just that you were babbling on and on about Buford and Tweetie."

"I *was*?"

"You were raving like a lunatic." C.J. touched my cheek gently. "Are you all right?"

"I'm fine. Just tell me that you didn't confess to a murder."

"She did," Edith said triumphantly. Between

you and me I wanted to take Edith's diamonds and shove them down her wrinkled brown throat.

"I'm not talking to you." I turned to my friend. "C.J., is that true?"

"Just a minute," Sheriff Thompson said. "Are you aware that anything you say can be held against you in a court of law?"

C.J. nodded dismally. Tears streamed down her face. It was a crying shame she hadn't taken the time to wash her hair since yesterday's ride in Tradd's convertible. Stringy hair is no way to start a prison stay—or so I've been told.

It is a fact that tall people get more respect than we vertically challenged. I, unfairly, am often treated as a child. There is really nothing I can do about it; with my size-four feet I can only wear so much heel. Still, I did what little I could and stood as straight as a yardstick, although of course taller.

"Sheriff, are you arresting Miss Cox?"

He smiled. "I'm not in the habit of arresting anyone for murder without first seeing a body."

"Ah, the body." The grande dame made a distasteful face. "I saw her myself, Neely. It's a gruesome sight." She turned to her middle grandson. "Tradd, dear, will you be so kind as to show Sheriff Thompson to Flora's room? You seem to know the way quite well."

Tradd had the decency to blush. "Yes, ma'am."

"I'm coming, too," I said, "and so is C.J."

Edith gasped. "You most certainly are not!"

"Habeas corpus!" I screamed. I wasn't sure what it meant, except that it had something to do with a body. Either that, or it was a town in Texas.

"*What*?"

"No one is arresting C.J. for a corpse she hasn't even seen, and—"

"She just confessed, you idiot. Of course, she saw the body."

"Well, I haven't, and I'm her best friend. Besides, C.J. didn't know what she was doing when she confessed. She didn't really mean it."

"Yes, I did, Abby."

"Shut up, C.J.!"

Sheriff put his hand up as if he were stopping traffic. "Who, here, has not seen the unfortunate Flora since her alleged demise?"

I was the only one to raise my hand.

"You can come, Miss—"

"Timberlake. Abigail Louise Timberlake."

He nodded. "I hope you have a strong stomach, Miss Timberlake."

"I've seen corpses before," I said, perhaps a bit too jauntily.

"Then, let's go."

The two of us followed Tradd to a small, windowless room off the kitchen. One actually had to walk *through* the pantry to get to it. This cubicle may have once been part of the pantry, but I had a hunch it had once served as quarters for some favored "house slave." It was hardly a bedroom for a free and salaried maid. At any rate, the grande dame was right, a gruesome sight met these weary eyes.

Only a teenager is capable of creating the mess that was Flora's room. Since the maid was well into her twenties at the time of her death, I can only surmise that she was emotionally stunted. That would have explained her involvement with Tradd. The tiny room looked as if a garbage truck had crashed into a section of Victoria's Secret. Bras, panties, and other assorted lingerie items were scattered everywhere, as were food wrappers and

containers. An empty Snackwell box adorned one
bedpost, a red lace brassiere another. A black, lace-
trimmed garter belt hung from the single-bulb light
fixture, red-and-white-striped candy canes dan-
gling from its clips. So distracting was the mess
that it took my eyes several seconds to spot the
body, which was lying in the open, right in the
middle of the bed.

"Oh, my god," I said and clamped a hand over
my mouth.

Tradd has hands the size of a catcher's glove,
and he clamped one over my eyes. "Grandmother
tried to warn you, Abby."

I yanked Tradd's hand away. "Just look at that
kris! The handle is exquisite—the intricate working
of the silver and the superb quality of those apple-
green jade insets."

"Abby!" Tradd was genuinely shocked.

I know, I should have been ashamed of myself—
I am ashamed of myself now, if that makes any
difference. So without further delay I will tell you
what else I saw. There lay Flora spread-eagled on
her rubble-covered bed, the kris buried in her chest
up to its exquisite, jewel-studded handle. Flora's
mouth and eyes were wide open in an unmistak-
able look of surprise. Curiously, there was very little blood.

"Oh, my," I said quietly. Although, as previ-
ously stated, I've seen my share of dead bodies, it's
not something I've gotten used to.

Sheriff Thompson went through the motions of
feeling for a pulse. Of course there was none to be
found.

He sighed. "Well, it appears she died very
quickly. There's no sign of struggle."

"How can you tell?" I asked. Then, as punishment, I bit my tongue.

Thankfully, the sheriff ignored me. He made several calls on his cell phone, speaking in a low urgent voice, while Tradd and I looked anywhere but the bed (okay, so I sneaked one last look at the kris). Then we filed out of the cubicle and back to the drawing room, where the grande dame and her descendants were cackling like hens who had just laid their eggs. Poor C.J. was the only calm one in the bunch. When we entered the room her brows raised slightly.

"Well?" Edith demanded.

"The girl's dead, all right," Sheriff Thompson said. He spoke to the grande dame, pointedly ignoring Edith. "Detective Lou Wingate will be right out. In the meantime, please make sure that everyone stays clear of the scene."

"I'll make sure," the matriarch said. "Does this mean you're leaving?"

The sheriff nodded. Then he looked at C.J. The poor girl looked like a raccoon caught in someone's headlights.

"You ready?" he asked gently.

C.J. thrust her hands out again. This time they were balled into fists.

"But you can't arrest her!" I wailed. "She's barely more than a baby."

"Ma'am, no one said anything about an arrest. But I am taking her in for questioning."

"No arrest?" Sally said indignantly. "Grandmother Latham, do something!"

"Sheriff Thompson knows his business, dear."

Edith was on her feet, her brown face muddy with rage. "But Grandmother, you heard her confess. She's guilty. She murdered Flora. The sheriff is supposed to arrest and cuff her. That's how it's done in movies."

"Sit!" the grande dame ordered. She turned to her friend. "Proceed, Neely."

"Are you ready, Miss Cox?" the sheriff asked gently.

"At least let her wash her face," I snapped. "In the meantime I'll go get her purse."

"I'm afraid I can't permit that Miss—"

"Timberlake. Abigail Timberlake. And *why* not?"

"Because she might try to escape, that's why!" Edith hissed.

"Shut up, Edith dear," the grande dame said through clenched teeth.

I would have expected someone, perhaps Rupert, to gasp, but the room was suddenly so quiet I could hear Edith Burton's wrinkles deepen.

"Ready?" the sheriff asked again.

The brave girl raised her chin. "Ready."

C.J. went docilely, and without cuffs. I wanted to ride with her in the sheriff's car, but he wouldn't let me. I considered making a fuss—the kind that might lead to an arrest of my own. It had been a day for slapping, after all, and if it worked for Zsa Zsa, it could work for me. One more slap and I could share the back seat with C.J.

Fortunately Tradd intervened. "I'll drive you," he said, putting a restraining hand on my arm. "I owe you that much."

"You're darn tootin' you do."

Tradd smiled. "You've got fire, Abby. I always did admire a woman with fire."

I burst into tears.

"Are you sure you're all right?" Tradd asked.

I had by then sobbed uncontrollably, blubbered

through a plethora of apologies, and honked my way through Tradd's handkerchief and half a box of tissues. Buford and I were never that intimate our entire first year of marriage.

"I'm fine, honest. I don't know what's come over me."

"I do."

"You do?"

The golden eyes shone, blessing me with their beams. "Let's see—oh, yeah. Your shop was gutted by thieves, you've been treated rudely by my family, and your best friend's confessed to killing my grandmother's maid."

I hiccupped. "She's not my best friend. Wynnell Crawford is. But, I guess you're right, it has been a rather trying couple of days."

Tradd pulled up in front of a long, low concrete building painted tan. "Well, we're here. Do me a big favor, Abby, will you?"

"You mean try not to get arrested, or worse yet, to do something that might land you in the hoosegow."

He grinned. "Yeah, like that."

Be careful, I told myself. You could get to like this man. Sure he had his faults—like driving too fast and lusting after Flora—but the latter was dead, and it is a fact that married men drive slower than single men. What mattered was that when the chips were down, Tradd was there. Greg, on the other hand, would have made fun of my red nose, and as for Buford, the man thought my tears were laced with anthrax, judging by his reaction.

We went inside where a very nice lady dispatcher named Stephanie explained patiently— several times—that no, I could not barge into Sheriff Thompson's office, but yes, I could use the phone if I kept it short and reversed the charges.

So I did what any self-respecting, middle-aged woman would do if given the chance. I called Mama.

Mama picked up on the first ring. "It's about time, Abby," she said, having accepted the call. "I'm going to Carolina Place Mall in Pineville with Dot and Marilyn. We're having lunch at the Olive Garden. They'll be here any minute."

I tried not to be annoyed. "Mama, this is important. When they come, tell them to wait."

"I can't."

"What do you mean, you 'can't?' "

Mama sighed. "Okay, so I'm not going to the mall with Dot and Marilyn. I'm going to your shop."

"*What*? Mama, did Greg catch the burglars? Are they returning the stuff?"

"No, dear, but it's almost as good. In fact, it's even better. You wouldn't believe the size of last night's crowd. Wynnell is there now, and she says that Channel 9 is on its way, and that the man from the *Observer* has already come and done his thing."

"What thing?"

"You know, the angel."

"Mama, *please*," I wailed, "I don't have time to talk about your visions. I have something very important to tell you."

"Oh, I know, dear. That's why I've been waiting by the phone."

"*What*?"

"You know I can smell trouble, dear, and ever since I woke up at six this morning my nose has been itching like there's no tomorrow."

Please, bear with me, but what Mama said was

undoubtedly true. The woman has a shnoz for news—good or bad. Ask anyone in Rock Hill. They'll tell you Mama predicted Doug Echols would win the mayoral race, and she didn't waver in her conviction even when Doug came in second in a three-way split. He won in the runoff, and had Mama taken her proboscis's predictions to a bookie, she would be a rich woman now and lunching somewhere in Southpark, not Pineville.

"C.J. killed someone, Mama. A maid named Flora."

"Nonsense, Abby."

"What?"

"That's not at all what my nose smelled. It smelled you, dear. You're the one who is in trouble."

"I didn't kill anyone," I wailed. "And I'm pretty sure C.J. didn't either."

"Pretty sure? You should be ashamed of yourself, Abby. After all that girl's done for you."

I bit. Blame it on the fact I was feeling weak and vulnerable, and didn't see how I could feel any worse. Blame it on the fact that I had yet to eat breakfast.

"What has C.J. done for me, Mama?"

Pearls clicked against the receiver of Mama's phone. "Shall I be blunt, dear?"

"Lay it on me, Mama."

"It's what she does for your image, Abby. Having C.J. as your friend makes you look good."

"How does hanging around with C.J. make me look good? She's a couple of sandwiches short of a picnic, Mama, or haven't you noticed?"

"Of course, dear. But you're a sandwich short yourself. Hanging out with C.J. makes you look more normal by comparison."

"*This* from a woman who wears pearls in the shower?"

"I didn't call just so you could insult me, dear."

"*I* called *you*, Mama," I shouted, and hung up.

"Abby, you all right?" Tradd tried to fold me into a sympathetic bear hug. Any other time I might have welcomed such a move, maybe even lingered a little to breathe in his cologne. Today, however, I was not in the mood.

I pushed myself gently, but firmly, out of his embrace. "I'm fine. Well, hell, no I'm not! I don't know what to do, Tradd."

He cocked that handsome head. "Geez, I don't know what to say. I live in Charlotte—only come down here to visit Grandmother—I don't know anything more about local lawyers than you do." He snapped his fingers. "Hey, there is a guy I went to school with. Not a lawyer himself, but I bet he knows a couple."

I slapped the receiver in his hand. "Call him."

"I can't, Abby. Billy's got an unlisted number, and I don't have it with me. But it shouldn't be hard to find him. It would have to be raining Persians and poodles to keep him off the course."

"Go get him. I'll wait right here."

"Uh—he plays at Litchfield Plantation Country Club. That's a good twenty minutes from here. By the time I find him and bring him back, it could be over an hour."

I ran that by my gray matter. "Go anyway. In the meantime, I'll make a few more calls back home. Somebody is bound to know the name of a good lawyer." I hoped Billy wouldn't be too mad if I'd already found one by the time Tradd returned.

10

"**W**ynnell's Wooden Wonders," the voice said cheerily, and then accepted the charges just as cheerily. Wynnell would never do that.

"This is Abby. Get me Wynnell." Perhaps I was a bit brusque, but Wynnell's new assistant, Lydia, suffers from chronic happiness. This wouldn't be so bad, were it not for the fact that the woman is a zealot, and will stop at nothing to bring a smile to one's lips. There are days when my lips prefer to remain absolutely horizontal.

It took at least five minutes for Wynnell to get to the phone, during which time I had to listen to Lydia singing along to a Captain & Tennille recording of "Muskrat Love." It must have been on cassette or disk, because no sooner did my torture end, than it started all over again. If indeed I do end up in hell—as some folks have threatened—I want five years knocked off my sentence.

Finally, a breathless Wynnell got on the line. "Abby, you won't believe what's going on over at your shop."

"Not you, too, dear! Wynnell, I really don't have time for flights of fancy. The most horrible thing has happened here—C.J. killed a maid."

"Was she a Yankee?"

"Wynnell!" The woman should be ashamed of herself. She has an unreasonable hatred of northerners. According to Wynnell the U.S. Immigration Service should transfer their focus from the Mexican border to the Mason-Dixon line.

"I don't know the victim's bloodlines," I wailed, "but she sounded local to me."

"Uh-oh. Then C.J.'s in trouble."

"Of course, she didn't really kill the maid."

"But you said—"

"That's what she's confessed to. But you know our C.J.: she couldn't step on a roach if it was armed with a gun and aiming at her ankles."

"You're right. Remember last year when she got head lice? She didn't shampoo for three weeks because she was afraid of killing them."

"Ah, so that explains it. Wynnell, listen, I need your help."

"Sure, Abby, anything. You're my best friend, so name it."

"Thanks, Wynnell. Say, you used to live in Georgetown, didn't you?"

"Of course. That's where I got married. Abby, you know that."

"And you and Ed lived there for a while, didn't you?"

"Three years, while Ed worked for the paper mill."

"That's what I remembered. So, here goes—I need you to help me find C.J. a lawyer."

"*Me*? You want me to help you find C.J. a lawyer?"

I rapped the receiver on the counter a couple of times. "There was a nasty echo, Wynnell. Yes, that's what I want. I was hoping you remembered the names of some Georgetown lawyers."

"Why should I remember any lawyers' names?"

"Well, I admit it's a slim chance, but what about the guy who did your will, for instance?"

"I don't have a will."

"Of course, you do! Everyone makes out a new will when they marry, silly, and anyway that's not my point. My point is—"

"But I *don't* have a will, Abby."

"You *don't*? What if you or Ed were to suddenly die? Who would get your estate? I mean, what about your children? What about *me*?"

"Oh, stop it Abby. Ed's not even sixty, and I'm as healthy as a horse. All this will talk is just plain unlucky."

Under better circumstances I would have read her the riot act. There is no excuse for not having a will. Any one of us could get run over by a cement truck tomorrow, or, like Daddy, dive-bombed by a seagull with a tumor in its brain.

I sighed. "Okay, what do I do now? Pick a lawyer at random from the Yellow Pages?"

"That would be a good place to start. Just make sure you pick a good lawyer—C.J. can afford it. I know she's young and, uh—well, a scoop short of a sundae—but she's a regular genius when it comes to money."

"I'm glad to hear that, but how do I find a *good* lawyer?" I will admit to being prejudiced in this area. But I was married to a lawyer, remember? Most of the lawyer jokes out there can ultimately be traced back to me.

"Perhaps I should restate that," Wynnell said quickly. "Forget about finding a good lawyer, find an *effective* lawyer." She paused. "Abby, if you really want to do C.J. some good, call you-know-who."

Wynnell is a Baptist and on the surface, at least, more religious than I. "Okay, so I'll pray," I promised, "but as they say, God helps them who help themselves."

"Abby, you're not hearing me."

"Yes, I am. The connection is just fine. Maybe a little static—"

"Call Buford!"

"*What*?"

"Now, you heard me. Listen Abby, I know you think the man is pond scum, but he's the best at what he does, and he's bound to know the best criminal lawyer in Georgetown County."

"The man is beyond pond scum," I growled. "He's the slime beneath the ooze beneath the sludge at the bottom of the pond."

"That may be," Wynnell said patiently, "but if you're really C.J.'s friend, you'll give Buford a call."

"Thanks for nothing," I snapped and hung up.

Okay, so I treated Wynnell shabbily, but that's what best friends are for. They're there for other reasons as well, of course, but if you can't mistreat your best friend now and then, and do so without fear of losing her, then she's not worth having. Wynnell knew that when I got back to Charlotte I would make it up to her. In the meantime I was able to work some of the panic out of my system, and replace it with pure, unbridled hostility.

That was exactly the emotion I would need for me to call Buford.

"Hello?" It was the Tweetie Bird.

"Tweetie, this is Abby. Let me speak to Buford, please."

"I can't, Abby. He's in the little girls' room."

"You mean little boys' room, don't you?"

"Uh—yeah."

"Reading the paper, I suppose."

Tweetie popped a bubble in her gum. By the sound of it, the wad she was chawing was big enough to produce biosphere.

"Yeah, how did you know?"

"I was married to him for twenty years, remember?" C.J. and I may be short a couple of picnic items, but poor Tweetie is missing at least one bulb in her chandelier.

"Buford won't like it if I disturb him, Abby. Not until he's done with the comics."

"Take the cordless phone to him, dear. Tell him it's a matter of life and death."

She trotted off, and I could tell from the echo of another popped bubble when she had turned the hall corner. I didn't need a bubble to tell me when she reached the bathroom door. Buford was his usual nasty self.

Five minutes later, Buford was on the phone. "This better be good," he growled.

"It's C.J. We're down here in Georgetown County at Latham Hall Plantation. C.J. has just confessed to murder."

"Holy shit! You don't mean she did Mrs. Latham in!"

"No, not her ladyship, but the maid."

"Flora?"

"You *know* her?"

"Uh—no. I mean, not really. I was at a reception the old lady gave—why the hell am I explaining this to you?"

"Funny, but Mrs. Latham never mentioned you," I said.

"It was a big reception and I didn't stay long. So, C.J. killed Flora, did she?"

"You know she didn't. That's why I'm calling you. You've got to help her out."

"Hell, I'm strictly a divorce lawyer, Abby—you know that. It wouldn't do a damn bit of good if I came down there."

"I'm not asking for you to come here, Buford. Just put me in touch with one of your local cronies—the best criminal lawyer you know in Georgetown County."

Buford had the temerity to laugh.

"It isn't funny, Buford. Now, who do I call? Better yet, you make the call."

"Get real, Abby. The best criminal lawyers in South Carolina live in Georgetown—the Triplett brothers—who just happen to be twins." He chuckled. "Anyway, they aren't going to waste their time on small fry like C.J."

"They will, if you tell them to."

"Abby, give me a break. I have a reputation to maintain. I can't waste good contacts on some psycho antique dealer."

"C.J. is not psycho! She's merely one food group short of a balanced breakfast. So, either you get those hotshot twins working for C.J., or I tell Tweetie about you and Flora."

I heard a gulp that could have swallowed Minnesota. "I'll talk to the twins," Buford said quietly.

"Good."

"And you'll keep your mouth shut about Flora?" It was as close to begging as I'd ever heard him get. Well, I'm not counting those times right after my babies were born, because my sex life is really none of your business.

"You swear *you* didn't have anything to do with her death, Buford?"

"I swear on my Mama's grave."

Trust me, that was Buford's most solemn oath. The man and his sainted mama were attached by the umbilical cord until her death the year before Buford and I met. From what I hear—not from Buford, of course—she was an itty-bitty woman with a tongue that could slice cold butter into neat pats. Come to think of it, that's why he married me; he still didn't have his mama out of his system. But he must have done a thorough job of mother-cleansing during our twenty years of marriage, because the Tweetie Bird and I are nothing alike.

Buford made the call to his lawyer friends and called me back within five minutes.

"Stay right where you are, Abby. The twins will be there in a minute. I got them on their cell phone. They're only about a mile away."

"Thanks, Buford. You really came through."

"Now, you come through for me," he grunted.

"A deal is a deal," I said calmly, "unless I ever get wind of you cheating on Tweetie again."

"I thought you hated her."

"I did, but not anymore. Tweetie's too dumb to know what she does half the time. You, on the other hand, had my heart. Then you stomped on it with both feet, and threw it in the trash. And as if that wasn't enough, you tore my babies from my bosom and gave them to that nitwit to raise. Lord, somebody could write a country-western song about the things you did to me."

"I didn't tear any babies from your bosom. Susan was ready to start college, and Charlie was a rising junior in high school." There was a long pause. "Abby, tell me something. If something were to happen to Tweetie—uh, I mean, if she and I were to split or something—would you take me back?"

"Not if you were the last male in the solar system," I said without a second's hesitation. "Why? Is something going on between you and the Bird?"

He hung up.

The Triplett twins were not at all what I expected. They were, however, very familiar. Classic white-bread looks, gleaming smiles, impeccably groomed, they could have stepped out of a magazine or catalog ad. They were absolutely identical—not even mirror images—even their own Mama couldn't tell them apart.

"Weren't y'all in that commercial?" I asked. "You know, that gum ad. Something about two tastes in one."

"Hey," one said, extending his hand, "I'm Daniel Chapman Triplett."

"Abigail Louise Timberlake," I said, "née Wiggins." When folks throw three names out at me, I see no reason not to counter with four.

"Gene Everett Triplett," the second one said in a raspy voice quite unlike his brother's. Frankly, it was rather sexy. "Call me 'Rhett.'"

"Call me Abby," I said, upping the ante.

"No doubt you're wondering why I sound this way," Rhett said.

Of course, he was right. "Bad cold?"

"I swallowed bleach when I was four."

"You don't say?"

"I made him drink it," Daniel said. "I told him it was magic juice. It could have burned his vocal cords beyond repair."

"My, y'all are certainly forthcoming," I said.

"We never lie, Abby," Rhett said.

Daniel frowned. "That's not true. We told Mrs. Lippman we would have her contract dispute settled by Monday, but we didn't have a ruling until Thursday."

"That wasn't a lie, bro. It wasn't our fault Hurricane Hugo came through."

I gasped. "Hurricane Hugo was over ten years ago. You mean you haven't told a lie in all that time?"

Daniel fixed his hazel eyes on mine. "You don't have to be smarmy to be a lawyer, ma'am."

"But—"

"We're smart," Rhett rasped. "We use our brains to navigate the system."

"It actually works in our favor," Daniel said. "Folks find the truth disarming."

I stared at them. "You're for real, aren't you?"

"Yes, ma'am," they said in unison.

"Well, I'll be." I was certainly disarmed. The *truth*! What an eccentric notion. And people say that mystery writer friend of Mama's—the one with the frizzy blond hair—creates characters too eccentric to be believable. Why, all one has to do is look around; the world is full of bizarre people. Except for you and me, of course.

"Has the sheriff booked your friend yet?" Rhett asked.

"Not that I know. He's been asking her a few questions." I nodded in the direction of the sheriff's office. "But they've been in there a long time. I'm really worried."

Then, for the first time in my life, I began to hyperventilate. It began as uncontrollable heavy breathing—not unlike sex—and progressed to the point where I thought I was going to rupture my throat. Or worse, stop breathing altogether.

"Somebody get a paper bag!" Rhett shouted.

Alas, the day of the paper bag is gone. Stephanie, the dispatcher, had only a plastic bag to offer. Fortunately the Triplett twins are indeed smart. Daniel ripped off his jacket, flung it over my head, and put me in a headlock. I'm not sure if it was the increased flow of carbon dioxide to my brain, or the smell of his cologne, but almost immediately my breathing returned to normal.

I struggled to free myself of the Armani prison. "Let me out! I'm okay!"

Daniel whipped the jacket off my head, nearly removing my ears with it. "You sure?"

"I'm fine. I just need to sit down for a minute."

They guided me to the row of faux-leather seats by the front door and made me sit. Rhett brought me a mug of water from the restroom, which I politely refused. Stephanie's lipstick was all over the rim.

"Jane Cox is just a baby," I wailed. "She's too young for the chair."

Rhett turned to Daniel. "Buford didn't say anything about a baby, did he?"

I grabbed Rhett's sleeve. "That's just an expression, you nincompoops." I drawled the offensive word to soften it; I am a southern lady, after all. "C.J. is twenty-four. I know she's a successful businesswoman and all that, but in some ways—actually, in most ways—she's very young for her age. But she's definitely not the type who would murder."

Daniel blessed me with a smile worthy of a TV commercial. "Abby, there probably isn't a soul alive who wouldn't commit murder if the circumstances were right."

"Could you?" I snapped.

"Absolutely."

"Me, too," Rhett said.

They were right, of course. *If* circumstances were right. Mama, wearing her pearls, would kill in a heartbeat, if it meant protecting me. I would do the same for her and my children. And maybe Wynnell. But Mama and I would only become killers if it meant saving loved ones' lives. We certainly wouldn't kill anyone simply because they were obnoxious. Neither would C.J.

"Someone has to have a motive to kill," I said. "C.J. had no reason to kill anyone in the Burton-Latham clan."

"So it might seem," Rhett said.

"What is that supposed to mean? She only met the gang yesterday—well, except for Tradd. She's only known him a couple of days longer."

"That you *know* of," Daniel said.

Contrary to some folks' opinion, I do not have a short fuse. My temper and my height have nothing in common. But this was just too much.

"The poor girl is innocent!" I shouted. "If all you can do is make innuendo, then thanks, but no thanks. I'll find C.J. another lawyer."

I jumped to my feet and headed for the phone.

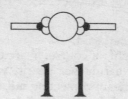

11

"We're sorry," Rhett rasped.

I turned and gave him the evil eye.

"Yeah, sometimes we get a little carried away," Daniel said quickly. "But you see, we refuse to defend a client we know is guilty. So we have to be careful."

I sat again. "Do y'all at least believe me? I mean, do you believe that I believe she's innocent?"

They looked at each other, and then nodded. "We believe you," Rhett said, "but we haven't even met the client. We can't agree to take her case until we've talked to her. After all, your husband said she confessed."

"*Ex*-husband," I hissed. "And yes, she did confess, but she was lying."

"Why would she lie?" Daniel asked. He sounded genuinely perplexed.

I shrugged. "Maybe she saw the murder happen. Maybe the murderer threatened her life if she didn't confess. Maybe she just—well, had a breakdown."

"Like a psychotic break?"

It was clear I needed to choose my words carefully. "What I mean is, maybe Jane *thinks* she did it—but she certainly didn't do it. Like I said, she didn't have a motive."

Rhett cleared his throat, but of course it did no good. "Look Abby, even if she just thinks she did it, she would still have to have a reason in her mind."

Daniel saw that I was about to bolt again. "But of course that reason wouldn't necessarily have to make sense."

I smiled gratefully. "Exactly. Maybe she didn't like the color of Flora's hair, so in her mind, she killed her. But in her *mind*, only. But even that is hard to believe. Like I said, her elevator might not go all the way to the top, but it's still functional."

They looked confused.

"Put it this way," I said, "in the pinball game of life, her flippers are a little farther apart than most, but she can still score points."

"Huh?"

"Never mind. So what do we do now?"

The brothers exchanged glances. Either they were able to communicate with their eyes, or they enjoyed looking at themselves.

"I'll take care of business at this end," Rhett said. "Daniel will drive you back to the Latham estate."

I swallowed my disappointment. I was beginning to find Rhett's scratchy voice attractive.

"But what will I do there?"

"Spy," Daniel said.

"On whom?"

"Everyone."

"Even the old—I mean, Mrs. Latham?"

"Especially the old crone," Rhett said.

"Guys, now you're being ridiculous. The woman is ancient—almost a century old. She couldn't stab an angel food cake with an ice pick. Besides, they all hate me out there. I have no reason to snoop around if I'm not with Tradd."

"Tradd?" Daniel asked.

"Oops. I guess Buford didn't fill you in on everything. Tradd's the hunky guy I'm with. He's my date for the weekend."

Their eyes swept the room. There were a few wanted posters tacked to a cork bulletin board, but Stephanie was the only other warm-blooded person in sight.

"Ah, he went off to see if he could find a lawyer," I said sheepishly. "I guess this could be awkward if he comes back with one, wouldn't it?"

"Don't worry," Daniel said, "if your friend prefers him to us, we'll gladly step aside."

"Hey, that wouldn't happen to be Tradd Burton?" Rhett rasped.

"As a matter of fact, yes. How did you know?"

They both laughed. "We used to call him Little Wet Tradd," Daniel said. "He was the scrawniest, goofiest-looking kid there was. Used to spend summers with his grandmother, who is a friend of our grandmother. We were driven over there almost every day and forced to play with him and his brothers and sister."

"Why Little *Wet* Tradd?"

"He cried a lot," Rhett said. "Of course it was our fault; we were pretty mean to him."

Daniel nodded. "Yeah, we were at that. It's because we were trying to get the attention of his older sister."

Rhett turned to his brother. "What was her name?"

"Edith," I said.

"That's it! Prettiest girl we ever saw."

"Edith and I once played 'doctor,'" Daniel said, blushing. "Of course, we were just little kids then."

Rhett punched his brother on the shoulder. "You did not!"

"Did, too. Remember how we always played hide and seek?"

"Yeah, so what?"

"Remember that time no one could find me? Not for hours and hours? Well, at least it seemed that way to me."

"Yeah, I remember."

"Well, I was hiding in this great big wooden chest in the boathouse. Edith found me and, well— you know."

"Get out of town," Rhett said, and slapped his brother on the back.

"Gross," I think I said.

"She still pretty?" Daniel asked.

"Gag me with a spoon," I said.

He scratched his head. "There was another girl, too—a cousin, I think. We used to call her Dog Face."

"Gee, you guys were a barrel of laughs."

Rhett snapped his fingers. "Alexandra! That was her name."

"She's still called Dog Face," I said. I know it was unkind of me, but this is a dog-eat-dog world, and I can be a bitch at times. The competition out there is fierce, after all. They say a hunk in the hand is worth two in the bush—or something like that— and I wasn't about to casually turn Rhett over to the beautiful Alexandra until I was sure I had no use for him in my bush.

"Oh, man, I'd like to see that Edith again."

I looked Rhett straight in the eye. "*You* drive me out there, and you might. I have to go pick up my cat anyway. But we still have one major problem: what's my excuse for staying there more than a few minutes?''

"Your things," Daniel said.

"What?"

"Your husband—I mean, Buford—said you came down for the weekend, right? So, you have things there, right?"

"Yes, but—"

"Just take your time collecting your stuff. In the meantime I'll renew some old acquaintances." Daniel winked at his twin. "Between the two of us we might come up with something."

"Lucky stiff," Rhett muttered, but he didn't argue with his brother.

Take it from me. Never date a man who can't lie. It was bad enough just driving in the same car with one. Halfway out to the Latham estate, on the private road, I checked myself out in the passenger-side mirror of Daniel's brand-new Lincoln Town Car. Having a jacket wrapped around one's head is seldom good for one's coiffure.

"Lord have mercy!" I cried, pressing back into my seat. "I look just awful, don't I?"

Daniel glanced at me. "Yes, ma'am."

"*What?*"

"Well-uh—I—uh—" he struggled with his damning tongue.

"Just spit it out, dear. I just read somewhere that pent-up veracity can be fatal."

"Well, your hair's all messed up, and that black stuff around your eyes is smeared. You remind me of that raccoon Rhett ran over last night on our way back from Charleston. But the raccoon didn't have lipstick on his teeth." He breathed a huge sigh of relief.

"Thanks," I said dryly.

We drove in silence for a few minutes. I am not the outdoor type—I find the open spaces in malls intimidating—but that morning the drive through the vast, uninhabited pine woods was food for my soul. Birds sang, the sun shimmered off the soft needles, and the pungent scent of sap filled the air, all regardless of what was going on in my world. Here there was order. Death, if not expected, was accepted. There is nothing like Mother Nature to dish out perspective.

"I suppose I've been overreacting," I said.

"No, you haven't."

I stared at Daniel. "What do mean?"

"You should be scared. Your friend, Miss Cox, is in deep trouble."

"But just minutes ago you said you and your brother could help."

"I said *might*. And that's only if she's innocent—"

"Which she is!"

"Yes, but even innocent people get convicted and punished. It happens more often than you probably think."

Until then I hadn't allowed myself to think beyond C.J.'s possible arrest. I certainly hadn't thought of a trial or, God forbid, *punishment*.

"Punishment? What kind of punishment?"

Daniel's hazel eyes seemed to light up from behind. "South Carolina has the death penalty, you know. Although it's unlikely they'll carry it through on a woman."

I was practically in shock. "It is?"

"Oh, yeah, nobody likes to kill a woman—legally, that is. Especially if she has a religious experience in jail. Your Miss Cox isn't already born-again, is she?"

"How should I know?" I wailed. "I'm an Episcopalian! C.J. and I don't talk religion."

He nodded. "That's good, then. If she was born-again, you would have heard about it. So, if she's convicted, we'll have her stage a dramatic jailhouse conversion. No state official is going to kill a sobbing woman with Jesus in her heart."

"I thought you didn't believe in lying!"

"It's not that I don't believe in it, Miss Timberlake—I'm incapable of it. I have no compunctions about encouraging others to lie. As long as it's for a good cause, of course."

"Like saving an innocent woman's life."

"Exactly."

A moment later we met the coroner's car—actually it was a dented blue pickup held together by rust and baling wire—returning from the scene of the crime. The dirt lane was barely wide enough for the Town Car, so Daniel pulled over on the sandy shoulder, and in the process mowed down several longleaf-pine saplings. The coroner did the same. Both vehicles stopped.

"Hey, Buster," Daniel said, lowering his window.

"Hey, Daniel. Where's Rhett?" The battered old truck didn't have glass on the passenger side, so there was nothing to roll down.

"Back at the sheriff's office, waiting to talk to his principal suspect."

I stiffened at the "s" word.

"And who's this pretty young lady?" Buster asked with a grin. Come Christmas Santa would have to bring him two front teeth *and* several molars.

"Remember Buford Timberlake?"

Buster shrugged.

"Big fat lawyer from Charlotte with beady little eyes like a snake? Always has dark sweat stains under his arms when he takes off his suit coat?"

"Don't hold back, dear," I urged.

But Buster was shaking his head. "Nah, those Charlotte lawyers all look alike." He grinned at me again. "But, like I said, who's this?"

I leaned toward him. "I'm Abigail Timberlake. Ex-wife, but no blood relation to the aforementioned reptile."

"She's an extremely short antiques dealer," Daniel said.

"Pleased to meet you, ma'am. My real name's Floyd Busterman Connelly, but folks call me Buster." I could feel his eyes zeroing in like heat-sensing lasers on my empty ring finger.

"Likewise," I mumbled.

"You going to be in the area long?"

"I don't think so."

Buster frowned, frankly an expression much more becoming on him. "Aw, that's a real shame. There's a whole lot to do here, you know? Have you seen the historical district yet?"

"No, sir."

"We got houses that date back to the mid-1700s. Blocks and blocks of them. Folks say we're a mini-Charleston."

"How interesting," I said. I wasn't just being polite, either. Where there're old houses, there are often old things—like at Latham Plantation Hall. *If* C.J. was incarcerated and I needed to hang around for a spell, I would at least check out the antique shops. Maybe even scan the classifieds in the local paper.

"I'd be more than happy to show you around, Ms. Timberlake. I've lived here all my life, and know a lot of interesting stories that you won't hear on an official tour."

"That's very nice of you, Buster, but I don't think I'll be around that long."

"Ah, that's a shame. I'm going to be having lunch at my Aunt Amelia's tomorrow. She lives in one of the oldest houses in Georgetown—1758— has the date on a plaque right on the front wall. Anyway, it's supposed to be a secret, but she's fixing to move into one of those retirement condos at the end of the year. She wants me to look over her stuff and choose what I want, before she puts it all up for sale. I was thinking maybe you'd like to come along and help me."

I reluctantly shook my head. "What a sweet invitation, Buster. But I really can't commit. Not until I know what happens to my friend."

As much as I appreciated his attention to my marital status, I was not interested. The man was simply not my type. Now, don't get me wrong and think that I eliminated Buster from my list of potential suitors simply because he lacked a full contingent of teeth. I am not that shallow—I once dated a man with no teeth of his own, although he had a beautiful store-bought smile. And I never would have known that wasn't his real hair if he hadn't gotten in the way of my shop vac when I was cleaning out my car. Not that that made a difference. Besides, if a smile was that important, I knew where to find C.J.'s cousin Orville. The best hog's teeth are hard to tell from first-rate dentures.

Okay, okay, I confess! I am prejudiced. Buster

was short. I could tell that just by looking at his arms. And I don't just mean short like Michael J. Fox, I mean *short*—like me! If I dated Buster we would be subjected to constant comments about what a cute couple we made. In the event we married, some well-meaning, but thoughtless friend or relative, would give us his 'n' hers step stools. What kind of foundation was that upon which to build a solid marriage?

Buster was no fool. He knew I knew he was sitting on a stack of phone books—in my case, it's the Charlotte Yellow Pages.

"Well, I'm in the book. If you change your mind, give me a call," he said.

"Thanks, will do," I called gaily. I am, after all, an expert on forced gaiety, a skill I honed during the months following my breakup with Buford. There was no point in making my children any more miserable than they already were, just because my heart was in shreds.

I'm not saying that Daniel was jealous of Buster, but for the rest of the way to the Latham manse he pouted in silence. Frankly, this was fine with me. Who likes to chat with a verbal time bomb? I can get all the insults I want from family and friends.

A wise Abigail, however, would have squared her shoulders, donned an invisible but thicker skin, and thrashed out a game plan with Daniel Chapman Triplett. A wiser Abigail would at least have spent those moments of solitude gearing up for the second shoe to drop at the Latham estate. Shoes come in pairs, don't they?

12

Edith answered the door. She made a poor substitute for Flora—even a real French maid would have been more polite.

"Yes?" she snapped.

"I'm Abby, remember?" I tried to push past, but her linebacker bulk prevented me.

"Who are you?" she demanded of Daniel.

"Daniel Triplett, ma'am. I'm here—"

"*Danny*? Little Wet Danny?"

Daniel turned the color of a maraschino cherry. "That's Little Wet *Tradd*. Nobody ever called *me* that." He took a step back, and I slipped behind him. "Who are you?"

"Edith, silly. You remember, Edith Burton—only now it's Edith Jansen."

"You're kidding!"

She shook her head, her broad face glowing like a two-candle jack-o'-lantern. She was wearing even more gold than usual, and I heard the faint tinkle of eighteen-karat hoops.

"Hey, I haven't changed that much, have I?"

"Yes, ma'am." Daniel bit his lip.

"I have? How?" Foolish woman—even Tweetie knows that's on the list of top ten questions a woman should never ask, and that's when dealing with a normal man.

"Well, uh"—Daniel struggled valiantly—"you've grown up, for one thing."

"*And*?"

"And, instead of looking like the sweet, young girl you used to be, you now look like this season's average recruit for the NFL."

"What?"

"Well, not exactly, of course, since they're guys and you're a woman, and I did say average—and no one person can resemble a group average, strictly speaking. But with those shoulders you could play one hell of a defense, and the last time I saw a neck that thick, it was attached to a bull."

"Well, I never!"

"Edith? Who's there?" I heard the grande dame call just as Daniel was about to get the door slammed in his face.

"No one important, Grandmother. It's just a tourist from Ohio looking for Myrtle Beach. I'm giving him directions."

Daniel peered down the hall—that is to say, he jockeyed to see around the hulking Edith. "Mrs. Latham, is that you? It's me, Daniel Chapman Triplett!"

"*Who*?"

Daniel repeated his full name.

"Ah, yes," the old lady said, advancing slowly. "Little Wet Daniel. Shirley and Otis Triplett's boy. There's another one of you, isn't there?"

"Yes, ma'am, my brother Rhett. But it wasn't *me* who cried all the time. It was Tradd."

"Nonsense. No Burton would blubber like that child did."

"No, ma'am, you're wrong. It was Tradd, for

sure." Daniel had his faults, but he was as brave as his biblical namesake. I'd sooner face a den of lions than an outraged octogenarian. A ticker that old has got to be a fragile thing, and this one had been through a lot already that day. At any moment, that ancient heart was liable to stop short, never to run again. It's not something I'd want on my conscience.

"Step aside," Genevieve Latham said to her granddaughter, who obediently and wisely stepped back into the foyer. That's when the old lady saw me cowering behind Daniel.

"You—child!"

I froze. Perhaps her vision wasn't as good as I thought. If I didn't move she might think I was Daniel's shadow.

"Abigail—that's your name, isn't it?"

"Yes, ma'am," I mumbled.

She had no trouble hearing. "Come in, child, and step lively. You too, Little Wet Boy. I may seem rich to you, but I can't afford to cool all of South Carolina."

We stepped inside. For the record, Daniel would gladly have let me go first, but I wouldn't let him.

"Have you no manners, young man?"

I squirmed around Daniel. "I'm sorry to bother you, ma'am. I just came back to get my things. I'll only be a minute."

"Nonsense."

"But it's true!"

"Stay as long as you like, child. I was hoping you'd come back."

"You were?"

She grabbed the sleeve of my T-shirt and tugged gently. Perhaps she meant to haul me one-handed along behind her. At any rate, I followed her to the drawing room, where she bade me shut the door. As for Edith and Daniel, as far as I knew they were still back in the foyer sparring—or, maybe even playing "doctor" for old times' sake. Nothing surprises me these days.

"Sit!"

I did as commanded, choosing an eighteenth-century carved Italian armchair. It was the only non-English chair in the room. It was also situated just far enough from the grande dame to feel safe (although, frankly, she was unlikely to catch her own shadow, even if given a head start), yet close enough not to appear rude.

"How's that little girl?" she asked.

"I beg your pardon?"

"You know, the one Neely took in for questioning."

"Ah, C.J.!"

"Yes, of course. Just wait until you're eighty-nine—you won't remember names either. At least not of folks you've just met. Now, things that happened seventy years ago, why, I can remember them just as clear as a bell. Take for instance the time my mama took me into town—well, never you mind that. You say the little girl—C.J.—is doing all right."

I shrugged. "Sheriff Thompson was still talking to her when I left. But I found her a lawyer—actually, two lawyers."

"Ah, yes, Little Wet Daniel and his brother. I heard they had become lawyers."

"And just in case they don't work out, Tradd went looking for a lawyer friend of his."

"Tradd?"

"He's really been super, Mrs. Latham. So have you."

"No need to be a sycophant, child. I like the girl. Grant you, she's a few clowns short of a circus, but she's sincere."

"That she is."

"Unlike my grandchildren."

Someone knocked timidly at the door.

"Yes?" the old lady called sharply.

The door opened just wide enough for Little Wet Daniel to insert his handsome head. "Ma'am, I need to talk to Miss Timberlake, if you don't mind."

Black eyes blinked. "But, I do mind."

"Uh—could you tell her my brother called and I need to get back to the station."

I started to get up, but the old lady waved me down with a single wrinkled finger.

"She heard you, boy. Is it an emergency?"

He looked at me when he answered. "No, ma'am. It's just that another client of ours up in Myrtle Beach—"

The finger waggled him into silence. "In that case, she'll be fine right where she is."

"Yes, ma'am." Little Wet Daniel ducked back into the hall and closed the door silently.

The grande dame turned to me. "Now, where were we?"

"You had just finished calling your grandchildren insincere sycophants."

"I did?"

"Or was it loathsome leeches?"

She smiled and leaned forward. "I don't think those were my exact words, but they're certainly true. All they want is my money—I know that. But, I don't really have much choice, now, do I?"

"I'm afraid I don't understand."

"Company, that's what. It gets lonely out here. You see, Abby, I never had many friends. Oh, sure, lots of acquaintances, but not many friends. I suppose I was too selfish with my time. Being a true friend takes a lot of time, you know."

"Yes, ma'am." Truer words were seldom spoken. Wynnell and I spend hours on the phone each week, and our shops are just across the street from each other.

"So, what few friends I had are all gone now. And so are my children—although I must confess, I didn't spend much time with them, either. Now it's just me and this great big house. You know what my grandchildren tell me?"

"No, ma'am." Frankly, I had a few guesses.

"They tell me to sell the house and move into one of those retirement communities. You must know the kind—first you live in a condo, then a one-bedroom apartment, which they call 'assisted living,' and then you're flat on your back in the nursing care unit. It's supposed to be a step up from your traditional nursing home."

"I see."

"Do you? Well, I don't. I can just as easily hire a staff of full-time nurses to live here. But my grandchildren have it all figured out—if I sell this place, I will have to sell most of my things. Between the sale of the house, land, and these"—she waved at the furnishings—"I'll have a lot of liquid assets at my disposal, even if I buy that condo in the retirement village outright. Not that I don't already have a lot of liquid assets." She looked me in the eye. "I'm a very rich woman, Abby. When I die, my grandchildren will be rich. But they don't want to wait until then. They're hoping I'll start divvying it up now."

"How rich are you?" I wanted to ask.

She read my mind. "How rich am I?" she said, and laughed. It was the sound of gold nuggets swishing around in a miner's pan. "I'm not as rich as Oprah, but *almost*. But, like I said, they can't wait for me to go naturally. They want to hurry my demise along by uprooting me. No doubt they hope the shock of my having to adjust to new surroundings will do me in."

"My mother is considering one of those retirement communities," I said. I was trying to be supportive. Really, I was.

"And you would let her do that?"

"Well—uh, Mama has a mind of her own."

"So do I! And I'm not budging. If I have to hire the entire staff of Georgetown Memorial Hospital, so be it.

"You go, girl," I said, "and I hope you live to be one hundred and ten."

"That's exactly what my grandchildren are afraid of. Old age seems to skip a generation in this family. All four of my grandparents lived well into their nineties. My parents, on the other hand, died in their seventies. And my children . . ." Her voice trailed.

We sat in silence for several minutes. "You know," she said at last, "only one of my grandchildren seems to love me for who I am. What would you say if I told you I am considering a new will in which I leave that grandchild everything?"

"You have another grandchild?" I asked innocently. "In Europe, perhaps?" I couldn't imagine any of the sniveling suck-ups I'd already met loved the old lady for herself.

She seemed to pale. "No," she said flatly. "All my grandchildren are right here. Now answer my question."

I shrugged. "Well, it's your money, but personally, I don't believe in inheritances. They're a terrible thing to do to someone you love."

The button eyes shone. "Explain, child."

"Say, just for the sake of argument, I was that special grandchild of yours—the one who loves you for yourself. There would be still be a part of me that would wish you were dead."

She gasped.

"*Subconsciously*, of course. And after you were dead—and I was rolling in moolah—that same subconscious part of me would be happy. Those negative feelings—even on a subconscious level—couldn't be good for my psyche. So, unless you want to do psychic damage to this favorite grandchild, don't leave him or her any money."

"Well, you certainly know how to lay things on the line."

"I do my best, ma'am."

She smiled cunningly. "So, child, what would you suggest I do with all my money?"

"You're asking *me*?"

"You mean you don't have any investment opportunities you want me to consider?"

I was aghast at the insinuation. "Mrs. Latham, I do not want your money! How dare you suggest that?"

My anger seemed to delight her. "So what would you suggest?"

"What did your mother die of?"

"Breast cancer."

"There you go. Leave your money to research. They might even find a cure for breast cancer by the time they run through all your dough. Your death might eventually mean saving the lives of millions of women world wide, rather than padding the pockets of pampered potheads."

She looked alarmed. "Do they smoke marijuana?"

I shrugged. "Who knows? But it alliterated nicely, didn't it? Anyway, you get my point."

She nodded soberly. "You make a lot of sense, child. I just might do something like that. Are the folks at the American Cancer Society the ones I want to get in touch with, or is there a separate foundation for breast cancer?"

Something crashed in the hallway. I distinctly heard the sound of breaking glass. Mrs. Latham stiffened.

"Shall I see who it is?" I whispered.

The woman had keen ears. She nodded, putting a finger to her lips.

"Keep talking."

To her credit, the old matriarch was quite skilled in the art of soliloquy. She made a smooth segue from breast cancer to her early childhood. As long as she worked her way up the ladder of her life, she had plenty to talk about. While she rambled, I tiptoed.

Small as I am, I normally make an excellent stalker. I have lots of experience, mind you, having been the mother of two teenagers and an unfaithful husband. But the centuries-old wooden floors of the Latham house would give Tinker Bell away. Every step I took, no matter how light and well placed, elicited a creak or groan loud enough to wake the dead in Los Angeles. Funny how I hadn't heard that racket before.

It was surely a lost cause by the time I reached

the door. Still, I flung it open dramatically, hoping to startle the eavesdropper into dropping something else, or, with any luck, having a mild heart attack.

But there was no one there. The hall was just as empty as Mrs. Hubbard's cupboard. I glanced down at the ancient hardwood floor and the threadbare Kazak at my feet. Not a shard of glass to be seen.

I hurried back to Mrs. Latham. "You don't have ghosts, do you?"

She cackled delightedly. "Every house this old has ghosts, child. But that was no ghost."

"How can you be sure?"

"Latham Hall Plantation ghosts have no reason to eavesdrop. If they want to listen in to a conversation, they come right in and plop themselves down on a chair. It doesn't matter if the door is closed, either."

"You're kidding, right?"

She shook her head. "I've seen it a hundred times. Especially the colonel. Why he—" She put a hand to her mouth. "You probably think I'm batty, don't you?"

"No, ma'am." I only hoped she didn't ask Daniel the same question.

"So, you'll stay the remainder of the weekend?"

"Yes, ma'am, if you really want me to."

"I wouldn't ask, if I didn't want you to. Now run along for a bit, I feel the need for a morning nap."

"Yes, ma'am." Now that I wasn't moving out, I didn't have to bother collecting my things. While the old lady snoozed I could roam the house with impunity. I could spy, as Daniel so eloquently put it.

She read my mind again. "Be careful, dear."

"Excuse me?"

"I would never accuse one of my grandchildren, of course. That's not what I'm saying, at all. But that girl—what's her name—"

"C.J.?"

"Yes, that's the one, she is no killer. Like I said, she might not have all her oars in the water, but she didn't stab Flora."

I breathed a huge sigh of relief.

"Now help me up the stairs, child. I'm suddenly very tired."

I helped Mrs. Latham up the stairs. She brushed off my suggestion that she install an elevator, or at the very least a mechanical seat. Climbing the stairs was her one form of exercise, she said. Her only fear was toppling over backward and breaking a hip, or worse yet, her spine. She had to have both feet on the same step before attempting the next, and she was swaying like a pine tree in a hurricane. By the time I got her to her room (she wouldn't allow me to put her to bed), I was ready for a nap myself.

Of course, I didn't pamper myself with a few hard-earned "Zs." Mama says there will be plenty of time for sleeping when we're dead—a sentiment I've often sneered at—but she has a point. In fact, there are very few things one can do in a coffin *but* sleep—unless you're Candy Woodruff, a girl I went to high school with. Candy was both a tramp and a mortician's daughter. The girl found more uses for a coffin, than a cook has for water—or so I heard. At any rate, as soon as I closed the door behind Mrs. Latham, I got right down to work.

I began my reconnaissance mission peering into the room next door, the bedroom that had been assigned to Edith and her husband Albert. I couldn't help but gasp. I should have known Edith would get the best room—she was the eldest, after all. But—and I know this will sound spiteful of me—all that beauty had to be wasted on a woman of her sensibilities. Sure, she had exquisite gold jewelry, and expensive clothes, but the woman probably wouldn't recognize a poem if the iambic pentameter jumped out and bit her. And that's exactly what this bedroom was—a poem!

Allow me to describe it briefly. The principal furniture consisted of a suite of painted Chippendale, in cream and emerald green. The four-poster bed cover was a rich cream and gold brocade, the bed curtains were green silk taffeta topped with a cream flounce. On the floor was one huge Bidjar medallion carpet with a cream background, and a green and rose floral border. The heavy velvet drapes at the windows were a dusty rose, lined with cream satin, and they complemented the carpet perfectly. A pair of French gilt armchairs had been added, almost as an afterthought, but they were the touch of genius.

I don't know how long I stood and stared—five minutes, maybe ten, when I felt someone tap me on my shoulder. I would have jumped out of my skin, but my jeans were too tight. Instead, I screamed.

13

"Shhh! You'll wake Grandmother Latham."

I glared at Albert Jansen. "What the hell are you doing scaring me like that?"

"Me? I come out of the bathroom and there you are, standing in the middle of my room, gawking."

"I wasn't gawking," I snapped. "I was appreciating."

He glanced around. "It is beautiful, isn't it? Edith tries to copy her grandmother, but it's either something you're born with, or not. Grandmother Latham was definitely born with it. She did all her own decorating, you know. No imported Yankee designers for her."

I nodded vigorously. What a relief to hear that her overbearing granddaughter was a failure. I always said that money couldn't buy taste.

"If I died right now—in this room—I'd go happy."

"I hear you."

I took a second look at the man. He was still plump and balding. His wire-rimmed glasses were badly in need of cleaning. He was an engineer for Pete's sake. Did there beat an artist's heart behind the expensive Italian leather pocket protector?

Like his grandmother-in-law, he seemed to read my mind. I suppose it shouldn't surprise me when people do that—large print is easy to read, after all—but it's disconcerting nonetheless.

"I never wanted to be an engineer," he said. "I became one because of my dad. He was one. If I had to do it over, I'd go to art school. What would you do?"

It is a question I've asked myself a thousand times, and each time I've come up with a different answer. Either I am the mother of all multiple personalities, or a fascinating woman, blessed with a vast array of interests.

"I suppose a gardener," I said. I must have been inspired by the floral motif of the carpet.

"Really? I love gardening, as well. Have you seen Grandmother Latham's?"

"No."

"Then come with me, I'd like to show it to you."

"That's very nice but there's someone waiting for me downstairs."

"Who?"

"A brilliant attorney who is going to prove that my friend C.J. did not kill your grandmother's maid."

Albert smiled. "If you mean Little Wet Daniel, he's already gone."

"He *has*?"

"Oh, don't worry, he said he'd be in touch with you as soon as he learned something."

He grabbed my arm. "I have something very important to discuss with you."

I was shocked by his behavior, but not too shocked to peel his fingers off my arm like they were the tentacles of a slimy octopus.

"Please." He was practically begging.

My mama didn't raise a fool—she raised *two* fools, Toy and me. Against my better judgment I followed him outside and to the garden.

It really wasn't much of a garden. Just a straggly hedge of boxwood planted in the outline of a heart. Inside the parterre a dozen or so badly spotted rosebushes strained for the sun, and in their midst, at the core of the heart was a flaking, whitewashed plaster statue of the Venus de Milo. Obviously Mrs. Latham preferred to keep her wealth inside the house.

We followed a weed-choked gravel path around the river side of the heart, and sat on a concrete bench, under a live oak, facing the water. Between us and the house was a screen of magnolias and cypress trees. Since the boathouse was on the other side of the mansion, this seemed like a very private place to talk.

This was as close as I had ever been to the Black River, and I was so charmed by its beauty that I temporarily forgot Albert's rudeness. The black opaque water made a perfect mirror. The trees and shrubs on the opposite bank were reflected in minute detail.

"It seems so mysterious," I gushed. "The water is so dark, it's unreal."

Albert pointed at a black bumpy log in the water not twenty feet away. "It's also full of alligators."

"You're kidding! That log's a gator?"

Albert smiled. "Alligators don't usually attack adult humans. Dogs and small children, now, that's a different story."

He didn't say just how small a child had to be before a gator showed interest, but I tucked my feet up under me just the same. Now that we were in the garden he seemed in no hurry to talk, but that was fine with me. Under the moss-draped oak it was cool. I could have sat there all day and watched the black water flow by.

"Hey," I said, emerging from my reverie, "why did the current stop?"

Albert chuckled. "It didn't. That's just an illusion. Since we're so close to the ocean, this is what is called a tidal river. For the past six hours the tide has been going out, and the river, which normally does have a weak current, looked like it was flowing rather faster. Now, the tide is coming in, but it's countered by the current. That's why the water looks like it's standing still, but it's actually rising." He pointed across the river. "See the mud banks over there?"

How could I not? They were as black as the river, but nonreflective. They reminded me of the herds of wallowing water buffaloes I'd seen on *National Geographic*.

"I see them."

"See that dead tree trunk sticking out of that one? The one that's tilted at a forty-five-degree angle?"

"Yes."

"See how the bottom two-thirds of it is black? That's how high the water will rise in the next six hours."

"Fascinating." I really meant it. Maybe if I played my cards right the old lady would ask me to stay on indefinitely—sort of as a home companion, a live-in curator, whatever. Just as long as I didn't have to clean bathrooms and mop floors. A little vacuuming never hurt anyone, and it would be a joy to dust her treasures.

I'm ashamed to say that my reverie was further disturbed by the rumbling of my stomach. "Has anyone mentioned lunch?" I asked sheepishly. "I'm afraid I haven't had anything to eat today."

"Ah, lunch on Saturday is usually a do-it-yourself affair. Saturday dinner, however, is the high point of the week—well, it usually is. But now with cook out of commission and Flora dead . . ." He shrugged. "Alexandra's offered to cook—she's in town now getting a few groceries—but between you and me, that woman can't cook. Not real food, at any rate. Just that frilly nouveau stuff that tastes like perfume."

"And omelettes." I jumped to my feet. "I'm sure your grandmother wouldn't mind if I helped myself to a little something now. She wants me to stay the weekend, you know."

"She *does*?"

"Is that so incredible?"

"No, of course not. It's just that with Flora's death, and all—well, and I won't know how to put this any more delicately—one would think she would find the presence of outsiders stressful."

If I had bit my tongue any harder the gator would have had an hors d'oeuvre. Contrary to public opinion my tongue is not large enough to make a full meal. At any rate, I counted to ten before speaking.

"We still haven't had that important discussion—unless this is it."

He took a linen handkerchief out of his pants pocket, removed his glasses, and wiped his brow. It was a melodramatic gesture unworthy of even a freshman drama student.

"It's my wife," he said.

"Go on."

"It all seemed so real back there in the house, but here"—he waved a stubby arm at the river—"it almost seems too bizarre to mention."

I sat down, cross-legged again. Come hell or high water, I was going to hear what he had to say. Stomachs can be filled anytime, but really good gossip is hard to come by.

"Tell me about it."

He glanced in the direction of the house. "I know you're going to think I'm nuts, but . . ." His voice trailed off. He shook his head. "God, I shouldn't even be thinking this. It's just too weird."

"Let me be the judge of that."

He took a deep breath. "I think Edith may have had something to do with Flora's death." He exhaled loudly and mopped his forehead again.

"Get out of town!" Okay, so maybe it wasn't an appropriate response, given the gravity of his statement, but I was plumb blown away.

He put his glasses back on. "You think I'm crazy, don't you?"

"No, I don't," I said quickly, "I'm just a bit taken aback. Please, Albert, elaborate."

"Well, I really don't know where to begin. I—uh—well—uh—"

"Begin at the beginning, dear."

His sigh was pitiable, the last whiff of air to escape from a crumpled beach ball. "I guess the beginning would be my marriage to Edith. This might come as a surprise to you, but I don't really fit into this family. Edith and I come from opposite ends of the spectrum." He paused, presumably giving me a chance to comment.

"I understand," I said cooperatively. "She came from a wealthy family of ancient lineage, and you were poor white trash."

"What the hell? That's not at all what I mean. Edith's family may be rich, but they have a bourgeois mentality. Yes, I know, I'm just an engineer, but I read. Three or four books a week. The last book Edith read was *Catcher In The Rye*."

"That's practically a classic. I read it in high school."

"My point exactly. She read it in the tenth grade. And she has no interest in art or music, either. Yeah, I know Grandmother Latham has a collection of antiques and art that will knock your socks off, but not so the rest of us. Do you know what Edith did with the money her folks left her?"

"Do tell."

"She took the Concorde to Paris, and then hired a limo to take her all the way down to Monte Carlo, where she lost more money gambling than I'll ever make in my life."

"But it was her money, right?"

"Strictly speaking, yes, but there are so many better ways she could have spent it."

"I see. So you're what Spiro Agnew would have called an 'effete snob.' "

He pushed up the wire rims and rubbed his eyes. "Your name-calling doesn't bother me. I'm just stating the facts."

"I'm sorry," I said sincerely, "it must be the lack of carbohydrates. Please, go on."

"Well, as you can imagine, my family was dead set against me marrying into the Burton-Latham clan. Edith knows how they feel about her—how can she not? Even my mama has a Ph.D., for crying out loud. As a consequence Edith has been extremely insecure in our marriage. Jealous as hell of any woman who even looked at me. You know what I mean?"

I nodded just to humor him. Contrary to some nasty rumors that have been circulating, I am not a shallow woman. I require my beaux to be more than just buff—brains are a definite plus. Maybe Albert Jansen had been blessed with a high-powered cerebrum, but he was totally without charm. I've seen store mannequins with more charisma.

"Sooo," Albert said, sounding like he was shifting into a low gear for a long haul up a steep hill, "it shouldn't have come as a surprise to me when she freaked out about Flora."

"You mean her death?"

"No, no," he said impatiently, "before then. Last night. Didn't you hear us? We had a terrible row."

"No, sir. Last night I was oblivious to the world."

"Well, trust me, we had one of our biggest go-arounds ever. She accused me of sleeping with Flora."

"Slut," I hissed.

He blinked. "She is still my wife!"

"I meant Flora, dear."

"Well, she did sort of come on to me earlier in the day. I was the first one downstairs for dinner—Edith can never make up her mind what to wear. Anyway, Flora came into the drawing room to serve me a drink, and then offered to remove a bit of lint from my collar. Only she got a little closer than she really needed to, and that's when Edith walked in and saw what Flora was doing."

"What you mean to say is that when Edith walked in, Flora was draped over you like a flag on a coffin at a state funeral, right?"

He squirmed. "Yes."

"That woman saw more traffic than the

Charlotte-Douglas International Airport. It's a wonder she didn't have landing lights installed on her stomach."

Albert was clearly shocked, and perhaps rightly so. One does not speak ill of the dead in the South, and my lips had been flapping like Panther pennants in a stiff breeze.

"Well, you have to admit she was a floozy," I said defensively.

"Yes, I guess so. I don't know why grandmother kept her on after what happened last year."

"Oh?"

"With Harold. But it was a one-time thing," he added quickly. "Miss Timberlake, please forget I said that."

"Harold, too?" Lord have mercy! That woman—" I clamped a hand over my mouth. After counting to ten in Spanish, I removed it. "Forgotten. So, you think Edith killed Flora in a jealous rage?"

He shrugged. "Edith doesn't have a violent bone in her body, but she was so angry—and then this morning Flora turns up dead. I'm afraid I don't know what to think."

"That's it?"

"What do you mean?"

"Angry words didn't kill Flora. Somebody stabbed her with a kris."

He removed his glasses, folded them, and jabbed one arm of the frames into his fancy-shmancy pocket protector. "Miss Timberlake, I—uh—sometimes have to get up in the middle of the night. Last night when I got up, Edith wasn't in our room."

"Oh, oh. At the very least she broke the contest rules."

"There's no need for sarcasm, Miss Timberlake."

"Sorry, but I'm starving, and we seem to be getting no place fast. Unless you sneaked downstairs after her and saw her plunge the dagger into Flora . . ."

He leaned toward me. I leaned away. It was a small bench, after all, and I detest conversations—especially with strangers, when I can feel their breath on my face.

"Actually, I was going to sneak downstairs, but before I could get my robe, I heard her coming. This might sound silly to you, but I jumped into bed. Anyway, Edith was panting when she came into the room. Her hair was—well, mussed up, and her nightgown was ripped."

"Maybe she was outside checking the boathouse again and somehow snagged it." I didn't want to get my hopes up.

"There's one more thing, Miss Timberlake."

"Yes?" My heart was pounding like a madman on a xylophone. Albert Jansen might well be the key to C.J.'s release.

"There was blood on her nightgown," he whispered.

14

"**A**re you *sure*?"

"Positive. The first things she did was go into the bathroom and wash the nightgown. When she got into bed she was wearing another one."

"Wait a minute. How could you see all that—the messy hair and the blood—in the dark?"

He scooted sideways on the bench, and I had no choice but to hop off. "But the room wasn't dark, you see. Edith is afraid of the dark. We always sleep with the bathroom light on."

I could very easily believe that someone as hulking and belligerent as Edith would be afraid of the dark. Buford was terrified of insects, after all. Once, as a gag, I gave him a tequila-flavored lollipop with a worm inside. When he took off the wrapper he nearly fainted.

"Why are you telling *me* this? And why now? My friend C.J. confessed this morning, remember? Why didn't you say something then?"

"Well—uh—like I explained, I've always been on the outside looking in, so to speak. I couldn't just bring this up, without talking to somebody else first."

"It's the sheriff you should be blabbing to, not me, dear." Suddenly I was furious. "You had no right to sit on this information, damn it! It's obstruction of justice. Don't you know that they could charge you with something."

"Like what?"

"I don't know—aiding and abetting, or something like that. The point is, it was wrong of you to keep that information to yourself."

"But you saw how Grandma Latham and the sheriff get along," he whined, "the two of them are thick as thieves. I want to be sure I'm not jumping to conclusions." He put his glasses back on. "Besides, I love Edith," he added in a small voice.

This was no time to lecture him on taste. "Come on," I said, and almost grabbed his hand.

We were halfway back to the house when we heard the car drive up. I must confess, that despite the gravity of the situation, and my extreme vexation, I found myself hoping that it was Alexandra returning from her shopping trip into town. Perhaps she had thought to pick up some bread and a package of pickle loaf. No doubt the Latham kitchen already stocked catsup. Flora wasn't going to get any more dead, or C.J. any deeper into trouble, if I indulged in a pickle loaf and catsup sandwich.

Both my heart and my stomach sank when I saw Sheriff Thompson's car parked in front of the manor house steps. The sheriff was still in it, but C.J. was nowhere to be seen. I sprinted for the car.

Sheriff Thompson got out to greet me. He looked as happy as a possum in a traffic jam.

"Where is she?" I demanded. The sheriff glanced at Albert, who was still trudging back from the garden, and not yet within earshot. "I'm sorry, Miss Timberlake, but Jane Cox signed a full confession."

"And you *believed* her?"

"Personally, I think something is rotten in the state of Denmark, but I had no choice but to book her."

"But why? You know she didn't do it, don't you?"

"Sometimes it pays for the mouse to play dead."

"What does a rat have to do with this?" I wailed.

He put a finger to his lips. Albert seemed to be walking faster.

"You mean you think *he* did it?"

"Look, we can't discuss this now. But believe me, Miss Timberlake, when I say you have a fine pair working hard on your friend's behalf."

I looked at him stupidly.

"Lawyers," he said quickly. "The twins."

I'm sure I blushed. "Yes, the Tripletts. My ex-husband said—"

The massive door to the house flew open, and out stepped Edith. No doubt she'd been watching us through the peephole, and couldn't stand being excluded from our conversation any longer.

"Why, Sheriff Thompson, how nice to see you," she boomed.

The sheriff tipped his hat, reconsidered, and removed it altogether. There was business to be conducted inside the house.

"May I have a word with you?" he called.

"Please, come in." She sounded almost gay.

I followed the sheriff into the house. By then pudgy Albert had caught up with me and was panting at my heels. Edith glared at me but held her tongue.

She led the sheriff toward the drawing room, but

then too had a change of mind, and opened the
door directly across the hall. It was the library. I
had seen libraries like that only in pictures; the
dark wood shelves from ceiling to floor filled with
leatherbound tomes, the enormous antiquated
globe, and the heavy Edwardian furniture, most of
it leather covered as well. And of course the ladder!

Maybe it's because I am vertically challenged,
but I have this thing for ladders. A hardwood ladder that rolls around the room guided by a track
is positively seductive. Therefore, I cannot be
blamed for trotting right after the sheriff with my
tongue hanging out, Albert still in tow. Now there
were two of us panting.

Edith loomed suddenly over me. "What are you
doing here?"

"I—uh—"

"I'd like her to stay," the sheriff said quickly. "In
fact, I'd like to see everyone."

Edith scowled. "Grandmother Latham's taking a
nap, and Alexandra is off shopping. I'll get the others."

Sheriff Thompson cleared his throat. "I want Genevieve to be here as well."

"Really, Sheriff!" She caught herself. "I mean, is
that really necessary?"

He nodded. "I'm afraid so, ma'am."

Despite her age, and the fact that she had been
awakened from a deep sleep, Mrs. Latham was not
the last family member to make an appearance.
Tradd, of course, had still not returned from re-
cruiting his lawyer friend, Billy, but that's not
whom I'm talking about.

"Where is that boy?" she said, tapping her slip-
pered foot impatiently.

She was referring to Rupert, he of the shiny
dome and pierced ear. According to Harold and
Sally, Rupert had last been seen rummaging
around in the attic.

"He wouldn't admit it," Sally said, "but I know
he was looking for the—uh—you-know-what."

Edith shot her sister-in-law a warning look.

"Ah, the treasure," Sheriff Thompson said.

Heads turned.

The sheriff winked at Mrs. Latham. "I've been
interviewing one of the players all morning. Of
course, I know about the treasure."

Sally, who was sitting on a high-backed leather
chair, crossed her arms. "Well, I think it's disgusting—I mean that Rupert is still playing the game.
Someone is dead, after all."

Edith arched a sparse eyebrow. "And what were
you doing all morning, Miss High-and-Mighty?"
she growled.

"Wouldn't you like to know, Miss Bossy?" Sally
snarled.

Frankly, I was shocked. We southerners maintain
a degree of politeness in public (mass murderers
excepted). Sure, we snap and hiss at each other
from time to time, but to snarl and growl, is practically unheard of. And name calling? That has got
to be a custom imported by latter-day carpetbag-
gers fleeing the Rust Belt.

Mrs. Latham was shocked as well. It was a good
thing she was sitting. She had turned the color of
cuttlebone and was swaying from the waist up.

"Children!"

"But, Grandmother! You've said yourself that
Sally is nothing but a vamp who got her claws into
Harold just so she could reel in the family fortune."

Mrs. Latham's mouth opened and closed several

times before any sound came out. "I most certainly did not," she finally managed to say. "Perhaps you misunderstood me. I said I found it interesting that our Harold would choose to marry a woman with certain financial liabilities."

"It's the same thing," Edith said triumphantly. She turned first to the sheriff, then to me. "Sally has a gambling problem."

Harold, who had been sitting with his chin in his hands, jumped to his feet. "Grandmother, this time Edith has gone too far."

The grande dame said nothing. The black shiny buttons were even shinier now that they were reflected through tears.

"Edith!" Albert said, on the old lady's behalf.

The eldest of the Latham-Burton grandchildren turned to her husband. I once saw a pit bull in Charlotte with much the same expression, seconds before he took a bite out of his master.

"What the hell business is this of yours, anyway? You signed a goddamned premarital agreement."

Albert, bless his pea-picking heart, looked just like the pit bull's owner the second after those nasty yellow teeth reduced his thigh by an inch.

Sally, meanwhile, was treating her sister-in-law to a cryogenic stare. I half expected Edith to shatter into a million freeze-dried pieces.

It was Sheriff Thompson, bless his badge-wearing heart, to the rescue. "Ladies and gentlemen!"

Sally continued to stare, and Edith mumbled something under her breath. The rest of us gave the officer our full attention.

"There has been an arrest made in the murder of Flora Dubois. Miss Jane Cox of Charlotte, North Carolina, is now in custody in the Georgetown

County jail awaiting a hearing to set her trial date. As for Miss Dubois, her body will be released to relatives following a complete autopsy."

Harold sat down again. "Did you say an autopsy?"

Sheriff Thompson turned to him. "Yes."

"But an autopsy isn't necessary, is it? I mean, we all know Flora was stabbed to death with a kris. Right?"

For some reason the sheriff glanced at me. "That would appear to be so. There are, however, certain findings that warrant an autopsy."

Sally found her tongue. "How does Flora's family feel about this?"

"At this point we have their full cooperation."

"Grandmother, do something," Edith whispered.

Mrs. Latham responded by closing her eyes.

"It just isn't right," Albert said softly. "Flora was a family friend."

I fully expected Edith to turn on her husband and accuse him of being more than a friend to the unfortunate Flora, but that was not the case. Not only did she affirm his assertion, she went on and on about how close the deceased was to the family—"practically blood"—she put it.

Sheriff Thompson merely shrugged and turned to me. "Miss Cox asked if you would pack a few personal things for her."

"What kind of things?" Surely in jail there were restrictions. C.J. might well like to wear her ball gowns in the big house, but I didn't want to make a fool of myself by packing them.

Mercifully, the sheriff had anticipated just such a question and handed me a list.

1. toiletries (shampoo, deodorant, toothbrush, etc.—NO makeup)

2. prescription medications (prescriptions must be included)
3. socks (4-6 pair)
4. brassieres (optional)
5. underpants (4-6)

That was it. No dresses, no slacks, no tops. And no makeup! I hoped the sheriff did indeed supply polka dot uniforms to his inmates. Without makeup a gal needs something to make her pretty.

I sighed, blinking back the tears. "Can do," I said, in a voice that sounded like I'd swallowed a frog.

It took me all of five minutes to gather C.J.'s essentials and stuff them in the overnight bag I brought with me. I grabbed my purse as well, since I intended to bum a ride back to the jail with the sheriff.

When I returned to the library, I found that the cast had been increased by one player. Tradd, handsome as ever, sat on the arm of his grandmother's chair, his own arm protectively around her.

"Hey, Abby," he said almost casually.

I thrust the overnight bag at the sheriff. "*So*?"

Tradd shook his head. "No dice. The guy I had in mind has a full caseload. But I hear Rhett and Little Wet Daniel are good. We used to play with them as children, you know?"

"Is that so?" I turned my back on him and faced the sheriff. "I'd like to ride back with you to the station, if you don't mind."

He bit his lip. "All right. We usually don't allow visitors until after the arraignment unless they're immediate family, but I guess an exception can be made."

"That's what exceptions are for," I said. I know, I can sometimes be too cocky—but it was either exude a little sass, or blubber like a baby.

"Are you ready?"

"Ready as I'll ever be." I waved my purse jauntily.

The Fabergé egg that flew out of my purse and landed on the Aubusson carpet was a complete surprise, I assure you. I do not tote million-dollar items in my pocketbook along with car keys, facial tissues, hand lotion, and other items I am too much of a lady to mention. If I were to transport something that valuable, I would stash it in my bra—people seldom look there.

Everyone gasped, myself included.

"She's a thief!" Edith barked. "Grandmother, isn't that yours?"

I gently scooped up the precious egg. Crafted of gold, with blue enameled panels, it stood about six inches high, including base. One of the panels had swung open to reveal a quartz replica of the czar's winter palace.

"Nicholas gave that to me," the old lady said wistfully.

I caught my breath. "The czar himself?"

She cackled. "Child, I'm not that old! Nicholas was my chiropractor—although he fancied himself my one true love. That was after my Elias passed on, mind you. Anyway, that's not a real Fabergé egg, child. But it's a nice copy, isn't it?"

For some reason Sally looked like she'd been slapped. "It *isn't* real?"

"Of course not. Even I'm not crazy enough to leave a genuine Fabergé egg lying around."

"But it doesn't matter if it's real or not," Edith screamed, "she still stole it!"

"Nonsense! I gave her that egg."

"But you didn't—" Edith clamped a brown paw over her own mouth.

The grande dame smiled tightly and turned to me. "Miss Timberlake, I told you to keep that out of sight until you got it home. Now look what you've done."

I hung my head. "Sorry."

She sighed. "Oh, well, what's done is done, I guess. Just remember, that may be just a copy of a famous egg, but it's still worth a pretty penny. You do have a good home-owners policy, don't you?"

There is nothing more endearing then an octogenarian taunting her greedy grandchildren. I was delighted to play along.

"Yes, ma'am. And I have an alarm on the cabinet where I keep my Lalique. I'll put the egg and the vase you gave me in there the second I get home."

Edith was turning purple. "*What* vase?"

The dreaded finger wagged at me. "Now you've really spilled the beans. That was a wedding present from Elias's mother. It was signed by René Lalique himself. I hope you haven't wrapped it up in a newspaper and just shoved it in your suitcase."

I stuffed the egg back into my purse. "No, ma'am. I plan to get some of that bubble wrap this afternoon."

"Grandmother, you can't just give your things away to strangers," Harold whined.

The ancient brows arched. "I'm eighty-nine years old—I can do anything I please."

Sheriff Thompson stood up. "On that note, I think I'll take my leave. Good day, Genevieve."

She nodded. "Keep me informed, Neely."

Without as much as a glance at the others, the sheriff strode from the room.

"You go, girl!" I said to my hostess, and then scampered off after the sheriff.

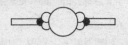

15

I could tell that the sheriff was a loving family man by the way he drove. Buford used to drive like his rear end was in flames until Susan was born. He was even more careful after Charlie's birth, and now that he has a bride with flammable body parts, he crawls like a snail through a glue factory.

"You're quite the little actress," the sheriff said before we had gone even a mile.

"Excuse me?"

"Sorry about the 'little.' That was just a figure of speech. As a member of an officially recognized minority, I should be more sensitive."

"No offense taken. I want to know what you meant by 'actress?' "

"Come on," he chuckled, "I know Mrs. Latham didn't give you that egg."

"How did you know?"

"It's my business, Miss Timberlake. That was a setup if I ever saw one."

"But I played it cool, didn't I?"

"Cool? You didn't miss a beat. There's a very frustrated and confused rat back there, who is no doubt foaming at the mouth as we speak."

We both laughed.

"You know," he said, "you could be a big help to me in my investigation."

"I could? How? You've already arrested your suspect."

He tapped a mental tune on the steering wheel for a minute. "Miss Cox confessed, so I was obligated to book her. But we both know she didn't kill Flora Dubois. Miss Cox might be—uh—"

"A flower short of a bouquet?"

"Yes. But she's no killer."

I breathed a huge sigh of relief. Mama claims that at that very second, the candles she'd placed around her bubble bath blew out simultaneously.

"So, what can I do?"

"I want you to act as my eyes and ears around that place. Snoop around—nothing obvious—and report back to me on anything you think will point to one of the grandchildren."

"You do think it's one of them?"

"It's not likely to be anyone from the outside. That old house is too isolated for any casual visitors, and Flora Dubois was a loner."

"Ha!"

He grinned. "Okay, so she had a bit of a reputation. But most, if not all, the men she's been involved with over the last several years were either members of the family, or their guests. She didn't hang out in bars."

"But she did hang out," I said, speaking ill of the dead for the second time that day. Frankly, I am surprised the grande dame dressed her in those skimpy uniforms. Perhaps she got a vicarious thrill from Flora's conquests. The elderly are not immune to urges of the flesh, mind you.

"Yeah, she did at that," he said almost wistfully. "She was definitely a looker."

It was time to change the subject before I learned more than I wanted to know. Sheriff Thompson was presumably a happily married man.

"Why don't you believe C.J.'s confession? I mean, beside the fact she's a float short of a parade?"

"Intuition. Years of experience. Take your choice."

"How do you know it wasn't me? Just because I'm petite, doesn't mean I'm incapable of stabbing someone in the chest. I am a good jumper."

He laughed politely at my self-deprecation. It is, after all, one of my most endearing qualities.

"All right. Here's the official scoop. But it is strictly confidential, so in a sense I am deputizing you."

"Do I get to wear a badge?" If so, C.J. and Wynnell were going to be intensely jealous. Even Mama might be willing to trade in her pink frilly apron and ubiquitous pearls for a silver star. At least, temporarily.

"No, I'm afraid not. Which reminds me, your cooperation in this case has also got to remain confidential. You must agree not to tell anyone about your involvement."

I held up my right hand. "I do so solemnly swear. So, what's the scoop?"

He laughed again. "Maybe I should make you take an oath promising not to be such a wise guy. But, okay, you saw the murder scene—what were your impressions?"

I thought hard. "Well—it wasn't very messy. I mean, there were no obvious signs of a struggle."

"Go on."

"Uh—well, there didn't seem to be much blood. I cut my finger slicing kielbasa last summer, and there was more blood than that."

"Exactly. You've got a good eye. So, what do you think that means?"

I ran a couple of episodes of *Murder She Wrote* through my head. "That Flora was killed some place other than her room, and that her body was moved there after she had bled for a good long while."

"You get an 'A,' Miss Timberlake."

"Abby, please."

"Abby. But, you're absolutely right. A chest wound—that kris was buried in her heart—results in a huge loss of blood. I'd say in this case, maybe 40 or 50 percent of the body's total. The coroner will be able to tell us exactly how much. At any rate, there would have been blood everywhere. I worked on a case once where there was blood even on the ceiling."

I shuddered. "Please, Sheriff, I'm feeling a little queasy. I haven't had anything to eat all day."

He nodded. "Sorry. How about we stop at McDonald's on the way to the station?"

"That's allowed?"

He laughed. "We sheriffs get to eat lunch, too."

"Sounds great, then, although I think I'll have the fish sandwich. But, since we still have a few miles to go, I do have one more question about Flora's blood. I guess it's kind of obvious, but all that blood had to go *somewhere*. Did you search the entire house?"

The sheriff stiffened. Undoubtedly I had gone too far.

"Oops, sorry," I said. "I realize you know your

job. It's just that—well—two heads are better than one, right?"

"Right," he said dryly.

We drove in silence for a few minutes. I looked out the window and prayed that his head was thinking constructively, and not brooding. He seemed like a reasonable man, but let's face it, sheriffs have a lot more power than antique dealers. The last thing I wanted was to share a cell with C.J.—especially if that cell was like the ones I've seen in movies with the toilet in the open.

Just when I could stand the silence no longer, and had a foot all ready to pop into my mouth, the sheriff cleared his throat. He tapped the steering wheel a few times.

"As I see it," he said slowly, "there are two possible scenarios. Either Flora was stabbed in a bathtub or shower, or she was stabbed outside during the rain."

"What rain?"

"That frog-strangler we had last night."

"Excuse me?"

"Ah, a frog-strangler is a really heavy rain."

I nodded. "My daddy used to call them gully-washers. But it didn't rain last night, did it?"

"Boy, do you sleep sound. The lightning was loud enough to wake the dead all the way over in China. And the rain! Whew! I turned on the porch lights, and it was like looking through a wall of water."

"But there aren't even any puddles," I wailed. "I pride myself on being observant, but what sort of unofficial investigator will I make if I can't even spot the aftermath of a toad-choker?"

He chuckled. "That's frog-strangler. And like I told you, you don't miss a beat. Of course, there aren't any puddles—you're in the Low Country now. There is nothing between us and China but absorbent sand."

"I see. So, *if* Flora was killed outside—in the rain—her blood would all have washed away."

"Exactly."

"And not even have left a trace?"

"Not after a rain like that."

"But there was *some* blood left on her. I definitely saw some blood around the kris."

"Yes, there was that. Maybe it wasn't hers though. That's another gap the coroner is going to have to fill."

"What about her hair and clothes?"

"What about them?"

"They were dry," I said triumphantly. "And her hair was combed—at least it wasn't very messy. Leave me out in the rain you described, and I'd look like a drowned rat."

He grinned. "Very good, Abby. I would have missed that part about the hair. It didn't look particularly messy, at that."

"And her makeup," I said, gathering steam, "she was still wearing makeup."

"Was she?"

"You bet your bippy. Now granted, she might well have been wearing a ton of waterproof liner and mascara, and she wore her foundation so thick even a tidal wave couldn't have washed it all off, but she was still wearing blush. The powder kind. It was all still there, in big clown circles."

"You noticed that in just a few seconds? What else did you notice?"

I shuddered. I had spoken ill of the dead for the third time. Mama says that if you badmouth a dead person three times in one day, bad luck is sure to follow. I'm not a superstitious person, mind you, but a large crow had appeared out of nowhere and was flying along the left side of the road just in front of the car. Perhaps I could undo—or at least neutralize—the trouble my tart tongue was getting me into.

"She had lovely legs," I said quickly. "That skimpy little uniform was very becoming on her. And I don't know when I've seen such a convincing boob job."

The sheriff said nothing, giving me a quizzical look. The crow, thank goodness, made an abrupt turn and flew into the woods.

"Well—uh—I don't swing that way. Not that there's anything wrong with it, of course. I just meant to say that she had some positive attributes."

He nodded. "Like I said, she was a looker. Well, if you can think of any other details, let me know. You've already been a big help, Abby."

"I have?"

"You bet your bippy." He laughed, then grew serious. "You know what this means, of course."

"That whoever killed Flora redid her makeup and fixed her hair?"

"Exactly. So we know it was a woman."

I smiled. "Not necessarily."

"Oh?"

"Well, I wouldn't be surprised if Harold has had a little experience applying makeup." I crossed my fingers to keep the crow away. "Besides, Flora wasn't exactly an expert in that field herself. Any man experienced with a putty knife could achieve the same results."

From somewhere deep in the woods the crow cawed, but I didn't see it again. Apparently one is permitted to speak ill of the dead to prove a point.

"And, anyway," I added, just to push the envelope, "Flora wasn't fat, but she was tall. And silicone weighs more than you think. I'd say she topped the scale at a hundred and fifty pounds. Now, I know we women are constitutionally stronger than you men, but when it comes to brute physical strength, we tend to lag a little. Brunhilde—I mean, Edith, might be able to sling a body over her shoulder, but both Alexandra and Sally would need help lifting a six-pack." I considered telling him about my conversation with Albert, but decided to keep back one card to play close to the chest. If I've learned one lesson in life, it is this: never ever trust anyone completely, except for your Mama, and even then, be sure and count the cash in your cookie jar before she leaves the house.

"I see," the sheriff said at last. "You know, Abby, you're really good at this. I almost feel that I should pay you for your observations.

"Enough to buy me that lunch at McDonald's?" I was broke after all. Broke and desperate.

He laughed. "Sure, lunch is on me."

After lunch we drove straight to the jail. The second I walked in the door the Triplett twins pounced on me.

"She won't cooperate," Rhett rasped.

"C.J.?"

"We told her to plead guilty," Daniel said, "but she won't listen."

"*What*?"

The brothers exchanged glances. Apparently it was decided that Rhett should speak.

"Your friend has changed her story," he said.

"Now she claims she didn't do it, and wants to change her plea. But—"

"But that's wonderful! I told you she didn't do it!"

More glances. "But she did," Daniel said quietly.

"Don't be ridiculous. You've both talked with her. You know she's not capable of murder. Now that she's finally come to her senses, it's y'all that aren't making a lick of sense."

Little Wet Daniel looked down at his shoes. "But there's the evidence."

"What evidence?"

Rhett pointed at the sheriff who was standing right behind me. "Don't you know? Didn't he tell you?"

I whirled. "Tell me what?"

Sheriff Thompson blinked. Then he swallowed hard. I hadn't noticed before, but he had one of those Adam's apples reminiscent of a fishing cork.

"We had plenty to talk about, Abby. I didn't see any sense in getting you more upset—not when there was a chance she'd changed her mind."

"So tell me now!"

There must have been a big fish on the line, because the Adam's apple jerked violently. "If you gentlemen will excuse us," he said, nodding at the twins.

"They'll do no such thing," I snapped. Trust me on this; I am a well-bred southern lady, and I know how to snap graciously.

He glanced around the reception area. "Then, let's at least go some place private."

Perhaps he had a point. There were others in the room now, including a couple who looked like they belonged to the senior citizen's chapter of Hell's Angels. Presumably they were there to see the sheriff, as well. Either that, or they were there to visit prisoners in the jail behind the building we were in. I scanned the faces of the elderly bikers. There didn't seem to be any resemblance between them and C.J. At least I didn't have to worry about them filling her head with nonsense if I delayed my visit a few more minutes.

I nodded. "Okay, your office. But this better be good."

The twins and I followed Sheriff Thompson through a door beside the dispatch window, down a long narrow hall, through a door on the left, and into a Spartanly furnished room. A desk, two chairs, and a gray, metal filing cabinet were the only furniture. Save for a photograph of Sheriff Thompson shaking hands with Governor Beasley, the plywood walls were unadorned. There were no windows. The linoleum on the floor looked like it had been used for ice-hockey practice, sans ice. The room smelled stale, underused.

"This is my inner sanctum," Sheriff Thompson said with a forced laugh. He closed the door. "This isn't my regular office, of course, but I guarantee you, no one can hear us here."

I tossed my head. "Fine, so shoot. I'm all ears."

He pointed to the chair facing the small desk. "Would you like to sit first?"

"What I would like is for someone to get to the point," I said through gritted teeth.

He took a deep breath, but to his credit, looked me straight in the eye. "The point is, Miss Cox's fingerprints were found on the handle of the kris."

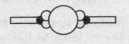

16

"**S**o what? It was clearly a setup. You saw what happened with the egg."

"Egg?" the twins echoed.

"Don't interrupt," I snapped. Again, it was a gracious reprimand.

"Well," the sheriff said, "there's more."

I tapped my foot on the scarred linoleum. "I'm waiting."

"The accused's fingerprints," he said carefully, "were found several places in Flora's room. Including the handle on the door that leads to the outside."

I snorted. "Again that means nothing. Like we discussed, Sheriff, Flora might have been killed in the bathtub. Now, if you had found her prints *there*, as well—"

He was nodding.

"You found C.J.'s fingerprints on Flora's bathtub?"

"Yes, Abby. But like I told you before, I personally don't believe the girl did it. Still, the evidence so far seems to point that way."

I sat down in the chair offered. "Poor C.J.'s in a peck of trouble, isn't she?"

Rhett took a cautious step away from me. "That's why we want her to stick to her guilty plea. You were right, you know. Miss Cox is a tune short of a songfest. If she pleads guilty, we might get her off on the insanity issue. But it wouldn't be temporary insanity, of course."

"You know we can't lie," Daniel said, as he wisely took a step away from me, "so we can't defend her as long as she pleads not guilty. We were hoping you could talk some sense into her. I mean, we tried, but—"

"And you two are the best Buford had to offer?" I roared. "She didn't do it, and she's not insane! Sure, she's a doughnut shy of a dozen, but aren't we all? In *some* way? Why just look at the two of you! You can't lie, yet you became lawyers. That's as smart a move as training a hen to hunt foxes."

"We wanted to become ministers," Daniel said sadly, "but they don't get paid very much."

"Well, thank heavens for that!"

"Mmm-mmm," Sheriff Thompson said, shaking his head. "I always did like a woman with fire."

I glared at the man behind the badge. "You are happily married, remember?" I turned to the Triplett twins. "Speaking of fire, y'all don't get to quit. Y'all are fired!"

Tears rolled down Daniel's cheeks. "We can't help it if we were born with scruples."

The mother in me wanted to hug the man, but the friend in me didn't have time for anything but business. "I want to see C.J., and I want to see her now!"

"Yes, *ma'am*," the sheriff said with a twinkle in his eye.

*   *   *

C.J. jumped with joy when she saw me. In fact, she jumped on my foot and nearly broke my arch. The sheriff, bless his soul, had permitted me to enter her cell, an experience I found fascinating.

"Well, dear, this isn't so bad. You have sheets, and the toilet is behind a screen."

"It wasn't always," said a deep voice behind me.

I turned and beheld one of the homeliest women I'd seen in a long time. She was as tall as two bean poles lashed together and as skinny as a celery stalk. She had a nose like a rutabaga, and virtually no chin. Her eyes were red and protruding, like radishes, and the bags beneath, which were too large to meet airline carry-on standards, were the color of eggplant. She was missing her two front teeth and the top of her left cauliflower ear. Her mousy brown hair was even stringier than C.J.'s, and if she didn't already represent enough vegetables, there was sufficient dirt under her fingernails to start a garden plot. This less than attractive package came wrapped in a faux python sheath of cheap polyester. The gold lamé sandals on her feet, however, were a nice touch.

"Abby, this is my new friend," C.J. squealed, clearly delighted to introduce us. "She's a fellow inmate."

"Pleased to meet you," I said, but did not extend a hand. If you ask me, this whole business of handshaking has gotten out of control. It was originally intended to show that one was unarmed, but now it has become the number-one method of spreading colds. We in the Episcopal Church ritually shake hands every Sunday in what is called "passing the peace," although more often than not it is really passing the virus. Imagine the discomfort of someone as hygienic as myself, having to listen to the wretched souls behind me wheezing and sniffing, and then at an appointed time be forced to shake their moist hands. Why not just press the palms of our hands together and bow slightly like they do in the Orient?

C.J.'s buddy thrust a gnarly mitt under my nose. "Name's Mozella Wiggins," she grunted.

C.J. clapped her hands in glee. "Abby, did you get that? Her name is the same as your mama's!"

"Not quite." I said, pondering the situation, "Wiggins is Mama's married name. Her maiden name was Humperdink." That was an out-and-out lie, but I didn't trust Garden Lady.

Mozella grabbed my right hand, which was still protectively at my side. Her fingers felt like artichokes.

"Why, ain't that something! Wiggins is only my married name. You ain't gonna believe this, doll, but Humperdink is *my* mama's maiden name."

"Get out of town!" C.J. squealed. "Abby, isn't that something?"

"That's something, all right," I said, and then impulsively gave her a big hug. The poor girl is an orphan, after all. It isn't her fault she was raised by a clan of kooks.

Mozella coughed. "Hey, you got a cigarette?"

"No, dear, I don't smoke." I turned to C.J. "I really need to speak to you alone."

"Oh, heck, Abby, you can say anything you want in front of Mozella. She's my new best friend— well, except for you, of course. And Wynnell. And your mama. And the Alphabet sisters back in Shelby."

"The Alphabet sisters?" I asked against my better judgment. I was under the impression C.J. had severed all ties with that fair city, except for occasional visits to see her grandmother.

"Well, their last name was really Grafton, not Alphabet. I just call them that to keep their names straight. Let's see, A is for Amber, B is for Betty, C is for Connie—"

"C.J., please! You have got to get a grip on yourself. What's this I hear about you changing your plea?"

"Well, I had to, Abby. Mozella, here, helped me figure out that I didn't kill Flora after all."

I whirled. "You did? How?"

Mozella picked something out of a clump of hair that was hanging in her face and twiddling her fingers, released it over the floor. I hoped to heaven whatever it was wasn't alive.

"I listened to her, honey. Apparently no one takes the time to *really* listen to her."

"But I listen to her," I wailed.

Mozella put her grubby paw to one side of her mouth and spoke to me as if C.J. were truly out of earshot. "Look, honey, she might be a couple of cigarettes short of a pack, but she's one bright cookie."

"I know that," I said hotly. "Not many other twenty-four-year-olds are successful antique dealers. But I still say I listen to her."

"Not really," said C.J. "Not like Mozella, here. Of course she's used to listening, on account of her business."

"Oh? And what kind of business would that be?"

"She's a sex therapist, Abby. She's been telling me all about it."

"Get out of town!" I said. "What do you really do for a living?"

"You see," C.J. said, "you don't listen."

"But I do." I turned to Mozella. "Are you a certified sex therapist?"

The radishes blinked. "A degree don't mean nothing in my line of work."

"I see. And I suppose you don't have a regular office either, do you?"

"Nah, that ain't legal in this state. But it is in Nevada, you know?"

I grabbed C.J.'s arm and hauled her clean across the room. "That's no sex therapist," I hissed. "Your new best friend's a lady of the evening!"

"Now, Abby, don't be jealous just because she makes a good living and you're broke. I know you wouldn't qualify as a sex therapist—on account of your problem with Buford—but Mozella is a professional magician, too. Maybe she could teach you how to do tricks."

"She's a prostitute, C.J.!"

C.J. recoiled in horror. "You mean she—uh—Lord have mercy!"

I nodded. "Yes, dear, that's exactly what I mean. Now what did you mean with that crack about Buford and me?"

C.J. turned the color of Mozella's nose. "Nothing."

I took a menacing step forward. I may be half her size and weight, but everyone knows it's all a matter of attitude. Dmitri, my cat, once chased a pack of dogs out of my yard and halfway down the block. Any one of those mutts could have made short shrift of my lovable fur ball—had he not had an attitude.

"Okay," C.J. said, putting her hands up in a defensive posture. "I heard that you were—uh—well, frigid. That you were never there for Buford."

"*What*? Who told you that?" Let me assure you, it was absolutely not true. Before Buford gained those extra sixty pounds, I was one hot mama. And even after the love handles developed into valises, I played the dutiful wife. It was only after his betrayal that the door to my love palace closed.

"Tweetie told me," C.J. said smugly.

"Tweetie is a liar! When I get back to Charlotte I'm going to—" I clamped a hand over my own mouth. As usual, C.J. had managed to divert me from the business at hand.

"Oh, Abby, please don't be mad at her. I wasn't supposed to tell anyone. And I wouldn't have, except that you were putting down my new best friend. And, anyway, I wouldn't dream of telling you what Tweetie said about your housekeeping skills."

I bit my tongue. "Well, we've somehow managed to get off track, dear. I'm definitely listening now, so tell me all about what happened last night, and how you first came to the conclusion that you stabbed and killed Flora, and then what made you change your mind."

C.J. smiled. She is really not an unattractive girl, and is intensely loyal, and thus would make the *right* person a good wife. Not that unattractive girls don't make good wives, but in C.J.'s case it wouldn't hurt to have a little something extra going for her.

"All right," she said, "I'll tell you everything. But this might take a while. Abby, maybe you should sit down—on account of your age and all."

"I'm forty-eight, dear. Willard Scott won't live long enough to wish me Happy Birthday."

I glanced around. Besides the toilet, which was

definitely out of the question, the only other furniture in the room was a set of bunk beds. I've always wanted bunk beds—perhaps it has something to do with me being altitudinally disadvantaged. At any rate, I would have happily perched on the top bunk, had there been a ladder. But, alas, there wasn't even a conveniently placed support bar upon which to step. Unless I asked for a boost, or hitched a ride with a hot-air balloon, I was out of luck.

Mozella must have read my mind. She trotted over.

"Top bunk is gonna be C.J.'s, on account of she's tall. Stretch, I call her. But you can sit on my bunk, if you like. Them sheets ain't dirty. They gave me clean ones just last week."

All right, so it was kind of her to offer. But the woman looked like she was host to more diseases than a third-world country. I forced a smile.

"That's very kind, dear, but I've been sitting all morning." I turned to C.J. "Now, tell me *everything*. Don't leave a single thing out. And I promise not to interrupt."

"Cross your heart and hope to die?"

"Stick a needle in my eye."

"Gross," Mozella said.

I nodded to C.J. to begin.

"It was a dark and stormy night," she began solemnly.

"*You* heard the storm, too?"

"Of course, Abby, but you're interrupting already."

"Sorry, dear, it's just that I didn't hear the storm."

"It was a real shutter-banger," Mozella opined. "Even I heard it in here."

I arched my eyebrows to communicate my displeasure at her uninvited participation in a private conversation. "Go on, Stretch," I said pointedly to C.J.

My friend took a deep breath. "Well, Abby, like I said, it was storming to beat the band, and I—uh, well, don't do too well in storms. Maybe it has to do with that time I got hit by lightning. Granny Ledbetter had sent me up on her roof to clean out the gutters, see, when this big thunderstorm came out of nowhere. I should have gotten down right away—I mean, I was already five at the time—but Granny had promised me a nickel for each gutter I cleaned, and the carnival was coming to town and I wanted desperately to see the two-headed billy goat. Have you ever seen a two-headed goat, Abby?"

I shook my head.

"Well, it was real disappointing. One of the heads was just a lump. It didn't have any eyes or ears, but it did have a nice beard. Both heads did—although not as nice as Granny Ledbetter's. Anyway, that's why I'm afraid of storms. Because of the lightning, of course. Not on account of the goat or Granny's beard. Does this make any sense, Abby?"

"More than you'll ever know, dear."

She smiled broadly. "Good. So, anyway, to calm me down, Granny Ledbetter used to make hot chocolate with—"

"Lots of little marshmallows?" You can't believe how hungry I was by then.

"Don't be ridiculous, Abby. I said 'hot chocolate,' not 'tomato soup.' Everyone knows you put those minimarshmallows in tomato soup. And you interrupted me again."

"I'm sorry," I wailed. I really was.

"Okay—but, this is your last chance. Now, where was I?"

These lips did not move.

"You were telling us how your granny put crackers in your cocoa," Mozella said.

"Yeah, but they have to be those little oyster crackers. Saltines won't do. Anyway, so I went down to Mrs. Latham's kitchen to see if I could find some cocoa mix and a box of crackers, when all of a sudden I heard her cry for help." She paused, and stroked her chin. "Actually, at first I thought it was a mouse squeaking, and, ooh, Abby, I hate mice. Did I ever tell you about the mouse I found in my lunch box in third grade?"

I nodded vigorously. It was a lie, I'm not ashamed to say.

"Oh. Well, anyway, I found some cocoa, and made myself a cup in the microwave, but I didn't find any crackers. I was just in time with the cocoa, too, because there was this real loud crack of thunder and the lights went off." She paused, perhaps for drama's sake.

"Go on."

"So, I was sitting at the kitchen table sipping my cocoa in the dark when I first heard the mouse squeak. Real high-pitched little cries, like this." She demonstrated in falsetto. "I tell you, Abby, I was about to run, but then it squeaked a couple more times and I figured out it was Mrs. Latham crying for help, and that she had to be in Flora's room. So I picked up the kris and—"

"Hold it," I ordered, risking her wrath, and losing her cooperation altogether. "Where *was* the kris at this time?"

"On the kitchen table."

"Who put it there?"

"I did, of course. Abby, I had a lot of cupboards to look through. You wouldn't expect me to hold on to the kris the whole time, would you?"

"Where was the kris when you entered the kitchen?" I asked with remarkable patience. Thank heaven I had all that experience interrogating my kids when they were teenagers.

C.J. rolled her eyes. "In my hand, where else?"

I slapped the palm of my hand to my forehead. "When and where did you first pick up the kris?"

C.J. paled. "I couldn't help myself, Abby. It was so beautiful—that gold handle, and all those gemstones. I'd never seen anything like it before."

"You *stole* the kris?"

Mozella clapped her filthy hands. "You go, girl!"

"I only borrowed it, Abby. I would have given it back, I'm sure. Only not right away."

I put my hands on my hips, a stance stern mothers have taken ever since the first cave woman caught her child playing with flint too near the tinder pile after one too many warnings. Like the first reprimanded cave child, C.J. regarded me sullenly.

"Shame on you, Jane Elizabeth Cox! Stealing is stealing. What would your granny Ledbetter say if she knew you had stolen that valuable sword from a sweet old lady like Mrs. Latham?"

"She'd tan my hide."

"You're darn tootin', dear. So think about your granny the next time you're tempted to steal."

"You're absolutely right, Abby. I should have gotten something for her. Granny loves presents."

"*What*? Didn't anyone ever teach you that—oh,

never mind! Now get back to your story. So you picked up the kris—which *didn't* belong to you— and then what?"

"Then I ran into Flora's room and stabbed her."

17

"You're sure?"

"Yes. You saw Flora lying on the floor with the kris sticking out of her chest."

I shuddered. The image was still very fresh. I could almost smell the sweet-musty odor of death.

"Yes, I saw her." I breathed deeply. "But, C.J., honey, just a minute ago you said you didn't kill Flora. You can't have it both ways."

The poor girl burst into tears and covered her face with her mannish hands.

"Now see what you've done," Mozella said accusingly.

"Oh, shut up," I said, causing generations of well-bred southern ancestors to simultaneously turn over in their graves. I swear the jailhouse began to rock.

"Why, I never!"

"I'm surprised 'never' is even in your vocabulary, dear."

"Please," C.J. sobbed, "don't be mad at her. It's me who's all screwed up."

I fished a wad of tissues out of my bra and

handed them to her. Don't get me wrong, I am not flat-chested, I just like to be prepared.

"You're not screwed up, dear, you're just confused. Did you, or did you not, stab Flora?"

"I don't know!"

Extracting information from C.J. is like tacking in a sailboat on a narrow canal. "Okay, let's say you did stab Flora. Then what? What did Mrs. Latham do or say? Was she hurt?"

C.J. shrugged. "I don't know. I guess not. She seemed all right this morning, didn't she?"

"But what about last night? Didn't Mrs. Latham say anything to you?"

"The funny thing is, Abby, I never even saw her."

"But you must have! You saved the woman's life, for crying out loud!"

C.J.'s head shook like the paint mixer at Home Depot. "Actually, I didn't see much of anything. It was blacker than Granny's coal bin in that room. All I could see were shadows—this big shadow choking this little shadow, so I stabbed the big shadow and then boom, the next thing I knew, the lights went out. That's all I can remember."

I slapped my young friend's cheek. Lightly, of course.

"Try to get a grip, C.J. You don't want to stay in here the rest of your life, do you?"

"What's wrong with here?" Mozella demanded. "The food is good and they got all the hot water you want."

"You might try using some—with soap!" I hissed.

To her credit—and much to my surprise—it was C.J. who steered us back to the business at hand. "Abby, I think someone hit me on the head."

"What?"

"Here, feel this." She pushed aside a hank of hair near her crown.

I gingerly probed her scalp, which, too, was in need of a good scrubbing. Sure enough, there was a lump the size of an egg—well, a pigeon egg at least.

"Ouch!" I said sympathetically. "This is pretty bad, dear. I think a doctor should see this. Did you get this last night in Flora's room?"

"In her bathroom. I went in there to wash my hands—they felt kind of dirty on account of I'd killed with them. But the lights were off, because of the storm, and I had to feel around in the dark. I had just found the sink—or was it the tub—when the lights in my head went out."

"The lights in your head?" If she meant what I thought she did, one could argue they'd never been turned on.

"Yeah, everything went black, and when I woke up my head hurt like the dickens."

"And then what?"

"Well, it only hurts now if I bump it."

"No, dear, what did you do when you woke up? When you came to?"

"I tried to get back in, Abby. But the door was locked."

"What do you mean by 'back in?' Where were you when you regained consciousness?"

"That's the really strange part. I was in the kitchen, sitting at the table again. Actually, I was sort of slumped over it, and my cocoa was spilled. The electricity was back on by then."

"But you went over to Flora's room and tried the door?"

"Yes."

"And when you found it locked, you didn't feel the need to call somebody? To wake me up and tell me what happened?"

C.J. hung her head. "This might come as a surprise to you, Abby, but I'm—uh—well, I'm a little bit different than most folks."

"Oh?"

"She means to say she's a tomato short of a salad," Mozella had the nerve to say.

I glared at Garden Lady. "Go on, dear," I said to C.J.

"Mozella's right, you know. I've always been a bit different. Not crazy, mind you—but I see things in a different way. Haven't you ever noticed?"

"Some people call that a sign of genius," I said, rather deftly sidestepping the issue, if I say so myself.

"*Really?*"

"Absolutely. Take Van Gogh, for instance. Or Robin Williams. Both geniuses, and both men with an unorthodox take on life."

"Robin Williams cut off his ear?"

"Not yet, dear," I said patiently.

"Wow, so I'm a genius. I always kind of suspected it, you know? I mean, sure a lot of people can read when they're two, but how many two-year-olds do you know who can do the *New York Times* crossword puzzle in ink?"

"None—and have it make sense. But C.J., dear, we seem to have strayed again. Why didn't you just come out and tell me what happened, when it happened?"

"But that's just it, Abby! I wasn't sure what happened. I thought maybe I'd fallen asleep over my cocoa and dreamed it all. When I discovered the door was locked, I knocked, but of course nobody answered. So I cleaned up the mess and went back to bed—by then the thunderstorm had stopped. Anyway, on the way back to our room I passed by Mrs. Latham's room, and there she was, snoring away just as peacefully as could be."

"You opened her door and peeked inside?"

"Don't be silly, Abby. This house has old doors, and they all have keyholes. I checked through the keyhole, you see. I'm actually very good at that."

"I bet you are. When Flora didn't answer her door, did you peek through her keyhole, too?"

"Of course! I mean I tried—I'm a genius, remember? But I couldn't see into Flora's room, because there was a key in the way."

"Hmmm."

"Wish I'da been there," Mozella muttered. "All you need is a paper clip. Straighten that sucker out and you've got the best lock pick in the world. It ain't nothing to push out a key and open a bedroom lock. Hell, them things was made to be jimmied."

I smiled thinly. Of course, at my age, and without collagen injections, that's the only way I can smile.

"You don't say, dear?"

"Yeah, picking them's like taking candy from a baby."

"I bet you're an expert at that, too."

"Well, I don't need to stand here and be insulted," Mozella huffed, but alas, she didn't budge.

"C.J., dear," I said, and put my hand on her shoulder, "what did it feel like? I mean, when you stabbed Flora?"

"Geez," Mozella said, "and you think *I'm* the lowlife!"

"That's not what I meant," I snapped. I tried to

push C.J away from the vexing vegetable, but she also seemed rooted to the ground.

"You know, Abby," C.J. said, her face lighting up, "that's a very good question, because now that I think of it, it felt kind of funny."

"Funny ha-ha, or funny odd?" Face it, with C.J. you never know.

"Funny odd. I mean, back in Shelby I once helped Granny Ledbetter butcher a sheep. This didn't feel like that, at all."

"You *stabbed* the sheep?"

C.J. grimaced. "Of course not! Granny made Elmer stick his head in the gas oven. But it was my job to cut him up afterward for chops and things. Stabbing Flora didn't feel at all like that."

"How did stabbing Flora feel?"

"Fluffy."

"Come again?"

"That's the best I can describe it, Abby. Flora was soft—like a marshmallow. Almost like air. Abby, that's why Mozella thinks I didn't do it. It didn't feel like I was stabbing a real person."

I pictured C.J. stabbing a giant marshmallow. Despite a fish sandwich, a large order of fries, and a large chocolate shake, I was still hungry enough to smell the damn thing.

"I see. And how many times did you stab Flora— or the marshmallow, or whatever it was?"

"Just one."

"You sure?"

"Positive."

I patted her shoulder. "Good girl. I'm very proud of you."

Mozella slapped her other shoulder. "Yeah, way to go!"

C.J. blinked. Her eyes were still puffy from crying. "Y'all are proud of me?"

"Of course, dear. You told me everything I need to know."

"I did?"

"You most certainly did, dear. And I think I can prove now that you didn't do it. You didn't kill Flora."

Mozella grabbed my arm again. "Y'see? I told you all you had to do was listen to her. And I was right, wasn't I?"

I wrenched free of Garden Lady's grasp. "As right as last night's rain, dear."

As much as I hate to be rude, I had no choice but to drag my friend across the cell, and then threaten Mozella with my shoe when she tried to follow.

"I'm not a murderess," C.J. chortled.

"I know, dear." I lowered my voice. "But don't tell anyone, including the sheriff, what you just told me."

C.J. gasped. "You don't trust him?"

"Honey, I don't trust anyone but myself, and sometimes I doubt the wisdom of that."

You could have landed a small plane on C.J.'s lower lip. "You don't even trust *me*?"

I thought fast. "I can always *count* on you, dear."

"Ooh, Abby, I love you!" C.J. threw her arms around me and gave me the granddaddy of all hugs.

"I love you, too, dear." To an outsider—and quite possibly to Mozella—it looked like a scene from a B movie.

Then I reached into the right pocket of my jeans and pressed the buzzer Sheriff Thompson had given me. It would have been much more fun to bang on the bars with a battered tin cup.

"So," the sheriff said, leaning back in his chair, "you learn anything in there?"

"Not really. That awful woman kept interrupting us."

He chuckled. "Adrianne's a case, isn't she?"

Adrianne? "Sheriff, is she dangerous?"

"Only to herself. Adrianne Menlow is what I call a one-woman crime ring. She turns tricks when she can, sells a little drugs, steals with some regularity, but never anything violent. She does, however, step on other people's toes. I expect to find her floating face down in the Black River one of these days."

"What's she in for this time?"

"Purse snatching. Some Yankee tourist got out of her car to take a picture of Adrianne's house—it's on the quaint side, by the way—and Adrianne came around the other side of the car and lifted her bag. The tourist is lucky Adrianne didn't take the car."

Fortunately, I had left my purse with the sheriff. It was still there, in the middle of his desk. I reached for it and patted it just the same.

"I see. Sheriff, poor Miss Cox has a nasty bump on her head. I think you should have a doctor look at it."

His face tensed. "Adrianne do that?"

I was tempted to tell the wrong lie. "No. C.J. fell and bumped her head while trying to reach the top bunk bed. You really need to put a ladder in there."

Trust me, no mortal doctor was going to get the

truth out of C.J. I mean, when's the last time a doctor's listened to you? *Really* listened?

"There used to be a ladder," the sheriff said wistfully, "but one lady inmate went berserk and decided to kill her cellmate with it."

"Not Adrianne?"

He smiled and shook his head. "The coroner had a good time with that one. Death by wrung neck, is how he put it."

"Sheriff, do you have Buster's work number?"

His smile froze. "Which Buster would that be?"

What an idiot I was! I had the temerity to warn C.J. not to blab, when the truth is, my lips are not only capable of sinking a ship, but the entire navy!

"Uh—the coroner. Floyd Busterman Connelly, I think it is."

"And why would you be wanting that?"

"Uh—he invited me to lunch tomorrow. At his aunt's house. I turned him down, but I've changed my mind. I thought his aunt might need some warning."

He nodded. "That aunt would be Amelia. She's a terrific cook. Be a shame to miss out on one of her meals—but that's not why you're hot to call Buster, is it?"

"I beg your pardon?"

"If you don't mind me saying so, you and Buster would make a great little couple."

I was too annoyed to be relieved. I snatched up my purse and stomped from the room—well, maybe stomping is putting it a bit strongly. When you are four feet nine and wear a size-four shoe, prancing is the best you can do.

At any rate, I pranced straight into the arms of danger.

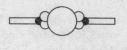

18

"Hey, good-looking," Tradd said, and I stopped in midprance. It was all I could do to keep from whistling.

He had changed from his morning's clothes, I'm sure of that, because he looked as fresh and clean as a daylily. Like a daylily, the top half of him was clad in orange, a color not usually suited to golden complexions, but Tradd was the exception. The bright cotton golf shirt made him glow. His cotton chinos weren't even creased behind the knees, so either he had changed in the restroom, or mastered the art of driving while standing. When you're that drop-dead gorgeous, no one is going to arrest you.

"Hi," I said, squeaking like a pubescent boy. "What are you doing here?"

"I've been remiss in my duties, Abby. I've come to take you to lunch."

I groaned inwardly. "Sorry, but I already ate."

"At the Purple Pelican?"

"McDonald's."

"Then you still haven't eaten. Come on." He grabbed my wrist and dragged me to the door.

Okay, that's not exactly the truth. I am pretty sure he touched my wrist with at least one of his golden fingers, and then walked in front of me to the door. I followed like a chunk of iron behind a magnet. The point is, I was powerless to do otherwise.

For the record, Tradd drove sitting, although for much of the way he managed to steer without the use of his hands. Or so it seemed. Not that they were on me, mind you, but as we sped along he gesticulated wildly, shouting the details of some story that was evidently very amusing, although the words were lost on the wind. Like an idiot I nodded and laughed periodically,

The Purple Pelican is located on Front Street in downtown Georgetown, a block south of the rice museum. It sits right out over the water, but the water in this case is not the Black River, but the Sampit. The folks in Georgetown are more modest than those in Charleston, and do not claim that the two rivers come together to form the Atlantic, as is the case with the Ashley and the Cooper.

The humble Georgetownians have built a charming boardwalk along this stretch of the river, and as it is lined by restaurants, galleries, and antique shops, it is an ideal place to while away a day. Indeed, were it not for the discordant presence of Georgetown Steel and the prevailing stench of a nearby paper mill, downtown Georgetown would have few rivals in the nation for ambiance.

Perhaps Tradd had called ahead for reservations, but it didn't really matter. The hostess at the Purple Pelican was as charmed by him as I, and proved it by immediately showing us to an outdoor table facing the water, with an espaliered camellia at least partially blocking the view of the steel plant. As we passed through the crowded main dining room I noticed a painted purple pelican prominently displayed on the mantel above a stone fireplace.

"What's with the purple pelican?" I said to the hostess after we were seated. "Aren't they really brown?"

The hostess was a buxom young woman in a tight-fitting uniform who just happened to bear an uncanny resemblance to Flora. Her name, however, was Barbie. I kid you not. At any rate, from the moment Barbie first laid eyes on Tradd I ceased to exist. Perhaps she never even saw me. Or perhaps she saw me and decided to treat me like a child. At any rate, I longed for a long pointed stick with a sign stapled to it that said SHORT, BUT STILL HERE. If the sign didn't work, I could always poke her with the stick.

"Well, that purple pelican is certainly unusual," Tradd said, bless his heart. "I've been meaning to ask about that."

Bodacious bosoms answered immediately. "Ah, that's Jake's idea. He's the owner. It's supposed to be campy."

"Where did he get it?" I asked.

Silence.

"I wouldn't mind having one for my beach house," Tradd said.

Well-endowed couldn't get the words out fast enough. "Jake's brother made it. He's a wood-carver. He has a studio out on Highway 17. I could show you where it is. I get off at three."

I know Tradd glanced at me, because what I felt was too short to be a hot flash. "Thanks, but I'm tied up for the rest of the day. Maybe some other time."

Humongous hooters was loath to leave. "That's our sixth one, you know. Customers keep stealing them."

"How?" I asked.

Barbie shrugged, but said nothing.

"How?" Tradd asked.

"Sneak them out under their coats, I guess."

"You're kidding!" I said. I couldn't imagine how someone could steal something that large and not get caught. My daughter Susan, I'm ashamed to say, stole a tape deck, by tucking it under her coat and pretending to be pregnant. You would have to be as tall as Brooke Shields and as wide as Roseanne to fit that pelican under an overcoat, and even then you'd look like you were carrying sextuplets to full term.

"I hope this table will be all right," our hostess said. Then inexplicably she threw her arms in the air and then dropped them to her sides, an action which caused her two best features to jiggle like a pair of Jello molds.

Tradd grinned from ear to ear, but said nothing.

"This will do just fine," I said. I was hoping the brilliance of those pristine caps would blind the little tramp—well, at least temporarily. Just long enough to make her stagger off the deck, over the boardwalk, and into the river. It certainly blinded me. But, alas, when I regained my sight, there she was, unabashedly searching Tradd's left hand for a wedding ring.

"Y'all enjoy your meal, now. Your waitress will be with you in just a minute," the hussy said, as her feet grew roots that pushed through the floor boards of the deck and down into the brackish water of the Sampit.

"Well, maybe you should run along now and seat someone else," I said, since Tradd no longer seemed capable of speech.

The hostess with the mostest didn't even hear

me. "Y'all let me know if there is anything else I can do."

"Scram," I said kindly.

"Huh?" Barbie said, still not looking at me.

"Put your eyes back in your foolish young head, and get back to work, dear."

That seemed to cut through her reverie. "*What* did you say?"

I smiled, drawing on the patience of my years. "Either you skedaddle, or I'm telling Jake you've been putting the moves on my man."

"Well, I never!" Barbie withdrew her roots from the floorboards and stamped back to her station. You can bet that Tradd's eyes followed her every wiggle.

No sooner had our butts touched our seats, than I laid into Tradd. "You," I said, "are a disgusting pig."

That got his attention. "Excuse me?"

"There is no excuse for your behavior. You eyes were all over that girl like white on rice."

He seemed puzzled. "She didn't seem to mind now, did she?"

"That's not the point. What about Flora?"

"Flora, what does she have to do with this?"

"She's dead for crying out loud! Murdered! Didn't she mean anything to you?"

"So?"

"So, don't you think it's a mite insensitive to be flirting with a restaurant hostess the same day your girlfriend is killed?"

He blinked. "Who said she was my girlfriend?"

"Well, it was perfectly obvious that something was going on, the way you two carried on. And her the maid."

"Ah, I see. So we're prejudiced, are we?"

I must admit to being grateful that outdoor dining section was enclosed by a screen. When I open my mouth that wide, I invariably get a snootful of flies.

"I am *not* prejudiced!"

Golden eyes danced. "In fact, I'll go a step further. Not only are you prejudiced against maids and restaurant hostesses, but you're jealous."

"Me? Of *what*?"

"Of my attention, of course."

I sputtered like a brush fire in a drizzle. "Why you—you—you egotistical cad!"

He laughed. "Cad—now that's a word one doesn't hear very often."

I would have gotten up and left the Purple Pelican right then and there had not our waitress appeared with a list of mouthwatering specials a mile long. Call me a masochist if you like, but I wasn't about to miss a meal I'd already paid for with my dignity. I ordered the most expensive thing on the menu and then excused myself to use the ladies' room.

On my way back to my seat and the insufferable Tradd, I just happened to glance at the TV above the bar. Much to my surprise, given the hour of the day, it was neither a sporting event or a soap opera, yet both the bartender and a few well-dressed patrons seemed engrossed in the show. I wandered over.

"Ah, CNN," I said aloud, reading the call letters in the corner of the screen.

"Shhh," someone said.

"What's going on?" I asked. "It's not that Saddam Hussein again, is it?"

"Shhh!"

Properly chided, I shut my mouth and watched as the camera panned a long line of people, some standing, some kneeling, on a sidewalk in a very familiar city. Columbia, perhaps? Raleigh?

"And these are only a few of the faithful," the handsome young moderator said, "this line extends down the street for four blocks."

I stepped closer. The street certainly looked familiar. Wasn't that—no, that couldn't possibly be C.J.'s shop in the background! Even if news of her arrest had reached the Charlotte media, it had nothing to do with the national scene, and why would there be so many "faithful?" Unless, those were friends and relatives from Shelby!

The moderator—Chet, I seemed to recall—moved rapidly down the line. "And now we approach the Den of Antiquity, a modest—"

"That's my shop!"

The chorus of "shhhs" sounded like a steam engine gaining speed.

"But it is! I'm the owner. You see, I'm just here for—"

"Can it, lady," the bartender growled.

I clapped my hand over my mouth and stared at the bizarre scene unfolding. Chet had entered *my* shop and was weaving his way through a crowd of the faithful—all of them on their knees now—to the rear wall.

"There!" he said, pointing solemnly at what appeared to be a blank wall, "is the so-called angel of redemption."

"I don't see anything," a smartly attired businesswoman remarked.

"Shhh!" I said.

"And right here," Chet said, shoving the microphone under Mama's face, "is the woman who first brought this phenomenon to national attention."

"Hey, y'all," Mama said, waving at the camera. Her first time on television and the woman was already a pro.

"Tell us, ma'am, how this was first brought to your attention and what you think it means."

"Actually, Chet," Mama said, taking the microphone from him, "this is the angel of the apocalypse, not the angel of redemption."

The crowd murmured.

Chet grabbed the mike back. "How's that?"

"Well"—Mama has strong, sharp nails, and Chet was a fool to tangle with her—"it's almost the millennium, right?"

"Of course. So what?" Chet was clearly irked at not being in control.

"So, that means the end of the world." Mama waited until the gasps subsided. "And this angel has been sent to warn us that the end times are nigh. Behold, the Almighty hath spoken." More gasps.

Nigh? Hath? Mama is a cradle Episcopalian, for Pete's sake. Where does she come up with that language?

Chet wrested the microphone away from Mama, but in doing so left some of his DNA behind in her nails. Chet's not all that bad looking, and I briefly considered cloning the clod.

"That's an interesting theory, ma'am, but back to my first question. How did this—this apocalyptic angel first come to your attention?"

"Shut the door," Mama barked.

"I beg your pardon?"

"Shut it!"

The camera swung around to face the door, and a very tall, thin, plain woman got up from her knees and attempted to close the door. This did not sit well with a short, squat, hairy man whose turn it was next to enter my shop. Tall, thin, and plain pushed, while short, squat, and hairy resisted. Mama couldn't have asked for a better setup. The two devout were almost equal in strength and the door went back and forth like a Ping-Pong ball on a very short table.

"Look!" someone in my shop shouted.

The camera swiveled again to the rear wall.

"See! The angel is flapping her wings!"

There followed a chorus of moans and religious ejaculations, the like of which would have made the most successful televangelist weep with envy. The commotion was too much for tall, thin, and plain, and her attention was diverted long enough for short, squat, and hairy to get the upper hand. The door flew open and stayed that way.

"Oh," at least fifty people moaned.

Mama snatched the microphone away from Chet, who had also let down his guard. "You see, that's what happened Thursday morning when I opened the door. The key had gotten stuck in the door and I was trying to jiggle it loose, and I looked up and there it was. Of course you might ask"— Mama waved the camera closer—"why I was even opening the door to an empty shop?"

"Ma'am—" Chet made a feeble and futile sweep at the mike.

"Because my daughter Abby was burgled, that's why—I mean, this shop was. Everything was taken. That happened Wednesday. I was here looking for clues because a certain Charlotte investigator, who shall remain nameless, but whose initials are G.W."—Mama leered into the camera— "was unable to come up with clues."

"Mama!" I gasped.

"Shhh!" No one at the bar even looked at me.

"Well, I didn't find any clues, but I did find the angel. And let me tell you something, the thieves who burgled my Abby's shop are going to pay dearly for their dastardly deed."

"Amen, sister," someone yelled.

Mama nodded approvingly. "Because, you see, the Good Lord hath chosen my daughter's shop to be the place of his final revelations."

"Hallelujah!"

"Glory be!"

Mama held up a hand for silence. "But y'all—the people of Charlotte, Gastonia, and Rock Hill—no, make that America—can be blessed by making a pilgrimage to the Den of Antiquity on Selwyn Avenue in beautiful Charlotte, North Carolina. Admission price to this holy shrine is only ten dollars per person, but y'all can get a family discount for—"

Apparently CNN was not in the mood to provide free advertising for Mama's latest harebrained scheme. The screen went momentarily blank and then lit up with coverage of a dingo roundup in Western Australia.

"Ah, shit," one of the Purple Pelican's well-dressed patron's muttered.

The bartender clicked off the set. "What kind of name is Den of Iniquity for a holy shrine?"

"It's Den of *Antiquity*," I snapped, "and it isn't a holy shrine. It's my antique shop."

Heads finally turned my way.

"My name is Abigail Timberlake," I said quickly, "and that was my Mama you just saw on TV."

"And I'm Tom Cruise," said the bartender.

"But that really is my shop!"

"Lady, you're not getting anything else to drink today. You've already had enough."

I wheeled and stamped off to rejoin Tradd. His chair, however, was just as empty as Buford's heart.

19

"**H**e just left," the waitress said. She paused. "I guess he thought you weren't coming back."

"*What?*"

She bit her lip. "Don't worry, I didn't cancel your order yet, and he already paid for both meals."

I may not have Mama's ability to smell trouble, but I can read faces pretty well. It's a useful skill in the retail business. At any rate, I sensed there was more she wanted to tell me. All I needed to do was to establish a connection. Her name, Youneequekah, filled her entire badge. It seemed like a good place to start.

"You have a very interesting name," I said. "How do you pronounce it?"

"*Unique-ah.* It was my mama's idea. She wanted it to be original. Someday I'm going to get up enough nerve to change it to something else. You know, something more ordinary like LaTisha or Tomika. My husband, however, is dead set against me changing it."

"Mamas," I said sympathetically, "can be a pain in the you-know-where. And so can husbands."

She laughed. "Tell me about it."

"So, dear, did the gentleman who was with me leave alone?"

She shook her head.

"That figures," I growled. "You wouldn't happen to know who it was he left with?"

"Oh, sure. He left with Barbie."

"The hostess?"

"She's the owner's niece. She comes and goes as she pleases."

"Probably steals pelicans, too," I said. "Keeps her daddy in business."

"Excuse me?"

"Never mind, dear. I was just being catty. If you bring me my lunch, I'll put something else in my mouth besides my foot."

"You want Mr. Burton's lunch too?"

"Gracious no!" Then it hit me. "You know Tradd Burton?"

"Girlfriend, everyone in Georgetown knows *of* Tradd Burton. Isn't he a fox?"

"He's gorgeous," I agreed. "Unfortunately he knows it."

"Isn't that the truth. Still, if I wasn't married, well—I guess I'd be tempted."

I cocked an eyebrow.

"Okay, so I'm tempted now. Aren't you?"

"Yes, and I'm ashamed of myself."

Youneequekah glanced around the outdoor pavilion. No one seemed to need her.

"There are probably more little Burtons running around this town than there are tadpoles in a swamp."

"You don't say!"

"Every time he comes down here to visit his grandmother, he—well, you know—finds someone new to be with."

"Yuck." I was remembering the touch of Tradd's hand against my skin. We hadn't, of course, become intimate, but still, you know what they say. When you have sex with someone, you are also having sex with everyone they've ever had sex with, and on down the line. In other words, I had thrilled at the touch of a thousand strangers—half of them women.

Youneequekah nodded. "Yeah, as far as I'm concerned, Tradd Burton is a 'look but do not touch' kind of man. Bet Flora Dubois (Youneequekah pronounced it *do-boys*) wishes she hadn't."

Shame on me, I hadn't even bothered to learn the girl's last name. Dubois! Maybe she really was French.

"Did you know she was dead?" I asked gently.

"You're kidding! I mean—no, I didn't know. When did she die? How?"

"Sit down, dear."

Youneequekah took Tradd's chair. "Tell me what happened."

"Last night—or maybe early this morning— Flora was killed. Murdered."

"*Murdered*? By who?"

"That I don't know."

"Does *he* know this?"

"Tradd? Of course. He found the body."

"Why, don't that beat all, and him sitting here like nothing happened."

I gulped. "I hardly knew the girl. Really."

"Oh, honey, I'm not blaming you. But him—he's the daddy."

"The *daddy*? He's Flora's father?"

Youneequekah couldn't help but snicker at my stupidity. Really, I was not offended.

"No, he wasn't Flora's father, he was the father of her baby."

"You mean—"

"Like I said, there are a lot of little Tradd Burtons running around. I call them Traddpoles."

"So Flora had a baby!"

"No, girlfriend, she didn't have it yet. From what I hear, she was due along about Thanksgiving."

"But that's less than three months from now!"

Youneequekah nodded. "Carried it well, didn't she?"

"It was her height," I said bitterly. Leave it to me to be jealous of a dead woman. But both times I was pregnant I looked like a cantaloupe with a head. A strawberry-size head. Mama disagrees, but I swear I showed within the first month.

"Yeah, it must have been her height. Of course I'm pretty tall, but when I was pregnant with Jamal, I showed more than that."

"Miss. Oh, Miss," a man called from a table across the pavilion. We both ignored him.

"So, you knew Flora?"

"She comes in to the Night Tide—well, she did— that's a club my Sammy and I hang out at sometimes. I've seen her there."

"Pregnant and still drinking?"

"We're not talking prime mother material here."

"Oh, Miss!"

Youneequekah glanced grudgingly at her customer. "Hey, I got to go."

"I know, but just one more question. You know a woman named Adrianne Menlow?"

She stood up. "Never heard the name before."

"Deep voice? Ugly as sin?"

"Several people come to mind."

"Looks like a walking vegetable garden?"

"Ah, you mean Addy! She's a friend of Flora's, and she's bad news."

"How so?"

"Drugs, prostitution—you name it, I bet she's done it. She shows up at the Night Tide, too, but usually manages to get herself thrown out. Ends up in jail half the time. The Night Tide isn't that kind of place." She stood up. "Well, too bad about Flora. Wonder who the old lady is going to name in her will now?"

"Excuse me?"

"*Miss!*" Both the man and his voice seemed vaguely familiar, but I am terrible at placing people out of context. Besides, I didn't know any men in the area outside of Burton-Latham men, and he certainly was not one of those.

"Hold your horses!" I called to the impatient customer. "Please explain," I said to Youneequekah, "about this will stuff. Are you saying Flora is named in Mrs. Latham's will?"

She shrugged. "That's what Flora had everyone believe. I didn't hear her say it myself, but that was the buzz. Apparently the old lady feels her grandchildren don't really love her—that all they want is her money. Of course, that's what Flora wants—I mean wanted—too. But at least she was honest about it."

"How terribly sad."

"Yeah, but can you blame the grandmother? Just look at Tradd."

"A loser with a winning smile."

Youneequekah snorted. "If it wasn't for those caps on his teeth, he'd have a smile like fish."

"That does it!" The customer, now irate, was on his feet and headed our way. Perhaps he was headed straight to Jake the manager to get Youneequekah fired. It was, of course, all my fault. I jumped up to intervene, and then suddenly it dawned on me why the man was so familiar. He was only my height, for heaven's sake.

"Oh, my gosh!" I wailed, "it's Buster!"

"Who?" Youneequekah—and I can't blame the poor woman—had taken refuge behind me.

"Buster Connelly, the coroner."

"Hey, I'm really sorry," I said to Buster.

"I bet you are."

It was a sour response from someone who had just consumed a free meal—Tradd's to be exact, and had been plied with enough gin and tonics to satisfy a congressional fact-finding team. Not to mention that I had carried his stack of phone books over to my table, which was the better of the two.

"No, I mean it. I don't know what got into me. It's been a crazy weekend."

"Yeah, yeah. You say no to my invitation, and the next thing I know I see you mooning all over that Burton kid."

"Believe me, I wasn't doing the mooning. Now, that cheap little hostess—"

"Is my niece."

"Oops. You don't happen to carve pelicans in your spare time, do you?"

"No, and Jake is not my brother—he's my brother-in-law."

"And I thought Charlotte was a small town. Well, you're not going to report Youneequekah's apparent inattentiveness to Jake, are you?"

"It would be a waste of time. Jake and I don't get along so well. I only come here because the food is good."

"And today it was free," I said pointedly.

Buster ignored me and started in on a slab of Girdle-buster pie, a specialty of the house. How he managed to pack so much into such a small space, was beyond me. Next time I took an extended trip I was going to ask Buster to pack my suitcases.

"Well, I'm sorry again," I said. "And I'm just going to keep on blathering until you forgive me."

"Will you reconsider my invitation for tomorrow?"

"Certainly not. I do not give in to coercion."

"Good, then I forgive you. I despise weak-willed women."

"Well, I loathe dictatorial men."

We looked at each other and laughed. Suddenly it didn't seem to matter so much that he lacked a few teeth. I mean, we all do at some time or another, don't we? Besides, like I said, C.J.'s cousin Orville could fix that in a jiffy.

He took a huge bite of pie. To his credit, he was able to speak without spraying me with crumbs.

"So, Ms. Timberlake—may I call you Abigail?"

"Please call me Abby. May I call you anything else *but* Buster?"

"No. Buster is going to have to do. Anyway, just what is it you want from me?"

"What makes you think I want something from you?" I snapped. "Maybe I have something to offer."

"Oh, do you now?"

"As a matter of fact, I do. I was hoping we could, uh—swap information."

He shoveled the last hunk of Girdle-buster pie into a mouth no larger than mine. Even David Copperfield could learn something from Floyd Busterman Connelly.

"I'm a government employee, not a news service.

I'm not in the habit of giving out information to just any old Tom, Dick, or Harry."

"My name is Abby, as you'll recall, and I'm not asking you to *give* me anything. I'm asking you to swap certain pertinent facts in the Flora Dubois case. Besides, you might say I already paid for this information with lunch." There was no need for him to know that Tradd was footing the bill, was there?

Buster glanced at the illustrated dessert card stuck in a metal holder in the middle of the table. "Okay. But it's going to cost you a little extra."

"How much extra?" I was broke, and almost desperate enough to steal a purple wooden pelican. Apparently there was a market for such things.

"Hmm. It's going to cost you coffee latte and a Key lime pie."

"You mean a slice of Key lime pie, don't you?"

"I mean a whole goddamn pie. It's to take to my aunt tomorrow. The latte is for here."

"Deal. Now, what do you have for me?"

He snapped his fingers, and Youneequekah, bless her heart, appeared out of nowhere. Clearly she was looking out for me. When she left with his order, Buster turned to me.

"You go first. You said we were going to swap facts along with the free lunch, remember?"

"Well, I've only got one fact, which, no doubt, you already know by now."

"Tell me anyway."

"Flora Dubois was pregnant."

He didn't even blink. "That's your fact? Ha, I didn't need to do an autopsy to determine that."

"So it's old news?"

"I don't mean to be crude, Abby, but all of Georgetown knew the second the sperm hit the egg. A Burton baby seems to have been Flora's goal in life."

"Slut," I said. I was speaking of Tradd. "Well, now, Buster, what do you have for me?"

"You have to be more specific. I haven't had a chance to give the sheriff a call—in fact, I'm not even done with the autopsy. Still, a few interesting facts have come to light. But you're going to have to fish for them with yes or no questions. I'm not at liberty to say a single word."

You have to admire a man who can pause for a lunch in the middle of an autopsy. "Okay, how's this—did Flora Dubois die from a stab wound involving a kris?"

He shook his head.

"Really?"

He nodded.

"But she did die from a stab wound?"

He shook his head.

"Poisoned, then stabbed?"

He shook his head more vigorously.

This was getting to be fun. "Smothered with a pillow and then stabbed?"

He stared at me.

"Am I close? Was a pillow involved?"

He nodded in astonishment.

"All right! Let's see—was she beaten to death with a pillow."

He gave me a pitying look.

"Of course, not," I said quickly. "Or else no one would survive summer camp. But a pillow was involved, right?"

This time he shrugged.

"Okay, so maybe it wasn't the pillow itself, but the pillowcase. Was she strangled by a pillow-case?"

He rolled his eyes.

"Oh, did I say *by* a pillowcase? I mean *with* a pillowcase, of course!"

He frowned.

"Well, then maybe it was something inside that pillow that killed her. Now what could that be—I know! She died of an allergic reaction to feathers, and *then* was stabbed with the kris?"

Essssssss. He sucked in his breath sharply.

Quite by coincidence Youneequekah appeared then with a cup of frothy cappuccino.

"I said 'latte,' " Buster growled. "This crap is all fluff."

That triggered something. "Fluffy. Think fluffy," I said to myself. I must have been speaking aloud as well, because Youneequekah gave me a worried look before disappearing again with the offending drink.

Then it hit me. "C.J. was tricked into stabbing a pillow!" I all but shouted. "And—because she's a piling shy of a pier—she was led to believe she had actually stabbed Flora. What did you do, find a bit of down stuck to the kris blade?"

He was beaming like a jack-o'-lantern. Given his dental state, I mean that literally.

"Damn, I'm good," I crowed. "So, someone else stabbed Flora and pinned it on poor C.J.—"

He had started to shake his head again.

"But you just as much as said so!"

He leaned forward and stared at me, like he was willing me to read his mind. It was a waste of time. Like I said, I'm good at deciphering facial clues, but unlike Mama, I can't see inside to someone's thoughts. Of course, I can read my children's minds, but that's only because the script changes so infrequently. At any rate, all I could see was a blank, sweaty forehead.

"You're close," he said, no longer able to restrain himself. "Now this is what really happened."

20

"Yes?"

"There was in fact a three-millimeter piece of down stuck to the kris blade, just beneath the handle—static electricity will do that, you know. So, yes, my guess is someone did trick your friend into stabbing the pillow. But Flora Dubois was not killed by a stab wound."

He paused to chase some Girdle-buster pie crumbs around his plate with the fork. I was tempted to grab him by his polyester lapels and shake the words out.

"Go on!"

"Well"—he licked the fork—"Flora was stabbed all right, but *after* she was dead."

"You don't say!"

He nodded. "She was shot first. A bullet to the head."

"Oh, my god!" I swallowed back an impulse to be sick. "But she looked all right. I mean, her head was still there and everything. Wouldn't a bullet have made a terrible mess?"

Buster sucked the fork tines clean. "It was a twenty-two-caliber bullet to the back of the head.

It left only a small entry hole, just ten millimeters in diameter."

"Speak English, man!"

"Uh—that's about a half-inch across."

"No exit hole?"

"Twenty-two-caliber pistols don't pack a lot of punch. The bullet ricocheted inside her cranium—tore up her brain real bad—but lacked the oomph to burst its way out."

I shuddered. "You make it sound like a live thing. The bullet, I mean."

He smiled pleasantly. At least *he* didn't have to worry about food stuck between his teeth.

"I've been doing this for eighteen years. I've come to respect the means of death, as much as death itself. Oh, sure, folks think a twenty-two-caliber bullet is just a glorified BB—but a BB in the brain can be just as fatal as a shotgun blast to the face. Just about anything can kill. Last week I did an autopsy on an elderly woman who suffocated when her pet mastiff sat too long on her chest. Two weeks ago it was a teenager who choked on a pencil eraser."

I nodded somberly. "My daddy was killed by a seagull."

"Ah, yes, birds and aircraft do not mix."

"Daddy wasn't in a plane. He was water-skiing on Lake Wylie when the seagull dive-bombed him. Daddy crashed into a pontoon boat and, uh—well, broke his neck. The seagull, as it turned out, had a brain tumor the size of a walnut. According to wildlife experts, it shouldn't even have been airborne."

"Wow!" His eyes shone with admiration. "I don't have any stories that top that."

I suddenly felt guilty. Trotting out Daddy's

death is not my custom, mind you. Why I needed to "one-up" a pint-size coroner is beyond me.

"Back to Flora Dubois," I said quickly. "So, she was killed by the bullet only? The kris had nothing to do with her death?"

"Not physically, at least. She was dead at least two hours before she was stabbed."

"You're sure of this?"

"It's my job," he said evenly.

"Of course, it is. No offense intended."

"None taken," he said and glanced at his watch. "How long does it take to make latte?"

I hoped a long time. I was actually enjoying Buster's company. Perhaps it was because I could relax with him; retire my feminine wiles to a back burner, so to speak. I know, it's a terrible thing to say, but there is something to be said for dating an unattractive man, and Buster was not easy on the eyes. Not that Buster and I were dating, of course—but if we were, I imagined we'd race go-karts, take walks in the rain, and eat funnel cakes while perusing flea markets. Wind, water, and grease are all things to avoid when out with a superficial man.

"I'm sure your coffee will be right out, dear. So, Flora was shot in the back of the head, then two hours later someone rolled her over and stabbed her in the chest. Right?"

Youneequekah appeared out of nowhere with a wink and a mug full of proper latte. Buster took the beverage without comment.

"Wrong. She was laid on her back soon after being shot. Blood had collected along her back, as well as the backs of her arms and legs." He slurped loudly. "There was virtually no leakage from her stab wound."

I willed my lunch to stay put. "But, she was

killed in her little room, right? Where she was found?''

Buster shook his head. ''I found particles of silica embedded in the entry hole and sticking to her scalp. My guess is the victim—I mean, Flora—was shot outside, and then drug indoors before the storm hit. Whoever shot her did a good job of brushing sand out of her hair, but they weren't thorough enough.''

''I see. And then the shooter—or possibly even someone else—tricked C.J. into stabbing a pillow.''

''No doubt it was easier than getting her to stab the corpse. But apparently one piece of the puzzle is still missing.''

''What's that?''

''The pillow. There was no pillow on the bed—stabbed or otherwise—when I removed the victim.''

''Funny, but I didn't even notice that. Then again, I'm not as used to seeing dead bodies as you are.''

''I should hope not.''

''But I have seen a few,'' I hastened to say. ''Anyway, since there was no pillow on Flora's bed, one might conclude that the pillow C.J. stabbed belonged to Flora. I mean, at least it went with her bed.''

''*Which*''—he slurped again—''would lead one to conclude that the second crime—it is undoubtedly against the law to stab a corpse—was not premeditated. But, you'll have to ask the sheriff about that.''

''Come again?''

''I'm only guessing that it's against the law to stab a corpse. I don't remember covering that in medical school.''

I may have blinked. I certainly didn't gasp.

"You're a doctor?"

"In South Carolina we have a dual system of forensic pathologists and coroners. The former are state appointed; the latter elected. As both a doctor trained in pathology and a coroner, I save the county a lot of money. But, this coroner stuff is only part-time. My day job is a staff position at Georgetown Memorial Hospital."

"Wow—I mean, well—I didn't realize you were a doctor, too."

"Ah, it's that old pickup, isn't it?" He pointed to his mouth. "Or maybe my lack of teeth? Maybe both?"

When caught with your pants down, there are two options as far as I can see. Either jerk those suckers up, or pretend you are making a fashion statement. Maybe even go ahead and take off your top as well. I decided to strip to the bone.

"You're right, it's both. I've seen better vehicles at the scrap-metal yard, and, well, you do look like your gene pool could use a little chlorine. I mean, you're a doctor, for crying out loud. You can afford to drive a Jeep Cherokee *and* visit a dentist!"

Buster sat back in his chair. "Never judge a book by its cover. You above all people should know that."

"What's that supposed to mean?"

"You may not have noticed, Abby, but I'm a little on the short side myself. So, I know what it's like to be treated as a child, just because one's head barely clears the counter at a teller's window."

"That happens to you *too*?"

He nodded. "And for the record, I was in the dentist chair, getting my bridge repaired when

Neely tracked me down. Tell me something, have you always been this shallow?"

"Who, *me*? Shallow?"

"I've seen parking-lot puddles deeper than you. And I thought we had a lot in common."

"But, we do!" I wailed. "I'm only shallow around strangers."

"Which is what we still are, apparently. And I'm not sure I want to know you any better."

"Does this mean lunch tomorrow at your aunt's is off?"

"You turned me down, remember?"

My cheeks burned. Why was it suddenly so important that Floyd Busterman Connelly like me? Because he was an unmarried doctor? Was I really that shallow?

"Well—uh—I reconsidered. I mean, you do need help going over your aunt's antiques before she puts them up for sale, don't you?"

He studied my flaming face. "You know, a doctor on staff at Georgetown Memorial Hospital— even one who moonlights as a coroner—doesn't make as much as a big city doc."

"I'm not asking you to marry me, for crying out loud! I'm trying to make up for being so rude."

"Is this an apology?"

"Yes."

Buster smiled broadly. So what was an incisor or two between friends?

"Apology accepted. I'll pick you up at the Latham Hall Plantation around noon."

"If I haven't been evicted."

"No need to worry about that. The old lady is genuinely fond of you and your friend. She finds your candor refreshing."

"She also loves my cat."

"That yellow-orange monster is yours?"

"His name is Dmitri, and he's very sensitive about his weight."

"Don't get me wrong, I happen to love cats—so maybe you and I really do have something in common—but—oh, never mind. Maybe she'll be more careful with your cat."

Buster may as well have leaned forward and said, "Pssst! I have an important secret I'm *not* going to tell you."

"What?" I wailed. "What does she do to her cats?"

"She tends to lose them."

"But, that's silly. Cats have a strong homing instinct. Dmitri could find his way back up to Charlotte if he had to."

Buster sucked air through what remained of his teeth. "She didn't misplace her cats. She lost them to those damn alligators in her backyard."

I shook my head. "Surely, you're mistaken. Albert Burton told me they're a danger to dogs and small children."

"And cats," he said softly. "They have a special fondness for sunbathing cats."

I leaped backward from the table so fast that not only did I knock over my chair, but I fell flat on my back on the hard wooden planks. In doing so, I somehow managed to take the tablecloth with me. Fortunately, Buster was holding his latte cup, so only the Girdle-buster pie plate went sailing.

"Abby, are you all right?"

I struggled to my feet. "Forget about me! It's Dmitri who's in peril!"

Despite Buster's attempts to make me count his fingers, and Jake's decree that I needed to ante up for a new latte cup—the airborne one having shattered—I was out of there in a New York minute. An alphabet-chanting Yankee couldn't have made it to the letter D before I reached the door.

. Not that my speed record did any good. I didn't have a car, and I wasn't up to sprinting eight miles to the Latham estate.

"Taxi!" I screamed stupidly. Even in a city the size of Charlotte, one generally needs to call for a cab.

"At your service, ma'am."

I looked up into the golden face of Tradd.

Why is it that a man will drive fast to show off, or when he's angry, but creep along like a snail when he's in a good mood?

"Step on it," I ordered. "You can gloat about your conquest later."

"There was no conquest. She was feeling sick so I drove her home."

"She didn't seem sick to me. Not physically, at least."

"She's pregnant."

"Slut."

"Hey, that's not fair! You hardly know her."

"I meant you, dear."

The golden visage dimmed. "I don't have to take this crap from you."

"Then don't. Because frankly Tradd, I've had all of you I can stomach for the weekend."

He seemed surprised. "It's that midget doctor, isn't it?"

"He's not a midget, and even if he were, he's ten times the man you are."

"That's a laugh." But instead of laughing, Lothario pressed the pedal to the metal, and I in turn was pressed against the seat, pinned there like a butterfly to a board by the G-force. The stupid top was down, of course, and my hair day went from worse to some place off the chart.

But to be entirely honest, although Tradd was a cad, he delivered me right to his grandmother's door. A man of lesser breeding would have turned around and redeposited me at the door of the Purple Pelican. Or worse yet, dumped me off by the side of the road. True to his heritage, Tradd even trotted around to my side of the car to open the door.

True to my baser nature, I opened the door just as he reached for the handle. "So," I said, "does this mean our deal is off?"

Tradd froze. "Uh—I don't think it does, do you?"

I allowed visions of a hundred grand to dance through my head while Dmitri, no doubt about it, languished in the belly of a gator. "A deal's a deal. We'd both have to change our minds. I, for one, haven't."

"I haven't either. But Abby, you haven't been looking very hard for the missing treasure, have you?"

I stood up, still in the Jaguar. That put us about eye to eye.

"*Me*? What about you? You spent the morning God-only-knows where, and then wasted precious time being ambulance driver to a round-heeled hostess. In the meantime, my second best friend in the whole world is languishing in the county jail."

"Hey, it's not too late to call this whole thing off."

Who knows? We might have done just that, had not the door to the Latham manse opened, and the lithe and lovely Alexandra stepped out onto the porch. At her heels was the bald and bare-bellied Rupert. They both seemed at first surprised, and then relieved to see us.

"Oh, there you are!" Alexandra cried, tossing her auburn hair. "You're never going to believe what's happened."

"Try me," I growled, and glared at golden boy.

"Edith just found the treasure—the missing antique. Isn't that wonderful?"

"Well, I'll be damned," Tradd said.

I sat back down in the car.

21

There was no one to blame but myself. It was as clear to me now as the handwriting on someone else's wall. I should have put my size-four foot down and forbidden C.J. to come down with us. I should have spent Friday evening conducting a systematic investigation, instead of obsessing on Tradd and Flora's relationship and Edith's rudeness. I really had no choice but to visit C.J. in jail, but I certainly didn't need to put on the feed bag at the Purple Pelican.

"So, what was it?" I heard Tradd ask, as though through a tunnel. "Not that old rocking horse in the nursery? I didn't see it around this time, but I didn't want to waste my guess on it."

"Oh, that old thing," Alexandra said, shaking her mane again. Perhaps her neck itched from all that hot, heavy hair. "It was all scarred and banged up. I don't see how that could possibly be worth a hundred thousand dollars. Funny, I didn't even remember it until just now."

Rupert shook his chrome dome. "It had a real leather saddle," he said wistfully. "I could ride that boy for hours."

I rolled my eyes and bit my tongue.

"Miss Timberlake"—she of the perfect jeans finally glanced my way—"you don't suppose a wooden rocking horse could be worth that much?"

I shrugged. I wasn't trying to be rude, but answering that was like asking a deaf doctor to diagnose a skin condition over the phone based on a blind patient's observations. It was madness. Actually, the treasure hunt itself was madness, and I was a raving loon for having gotten myself involved in it. If C.J. was a banana short of a split, I didn't even have the ice cream.

"Well, that all depends—"

The front door to the manse opened again, this time with a slam. Edith stood there growling like a gorilla in a Chanel suit. Her chubby hubby was nowhere to be seen.

"Tradd! Where have you been? Grandmother wants to talk to you!"

Golden boy remained immobile as an Oscar. "*Well*? Were you right? Did you win?"

Edith glared at me. I know, there are some who will contest my ability to discern a glare at fifty feet, but all I can say is, thank heaven I was wearing sunglasses.

"What is *she* doing here?" she shouted.

"Why, Edith," Alexandra said, clearly shocked, "she's grandmother's guest, remember?"

"She's Tradd's guest, you twit, and she doesn't belong here."

"You lost, didn't you?" Rupert, bless his West Coast heart, could not contain his glee.

Edith answered by slamming the door behind her. The woman was clearly blessed with upper body strength. It's a wonder the old house was still standing.

Tradd grinned. "Never a dull moment around

her. Well, grandmother beckons." He tipped an imaginary hat at me and trotted off to do the old biddy's bidding. Just between you and me, it is possible to admire a guy's buns *and* be spitting mad at him at the same time.

"Hope y'all don't expect me to stay out here and chew the fat," Rupert said quickly, "when the real show is inside." He darted after his older brother.

"So, that just leaves us," Alexandra said. "Good. I was hoping we'd have a chance to have a private chat."

"I'm flattered, dear." Indeed, I was. "But I have to find my cat, before the gators do. Have you seen him lately?"

Periwinkle eyes regarded me innocently. "Which cat would that be?"

"You've got to be kidding, dear. That big yellow cat your grandmother's been clutching like an overnight bag in a crowded airline terminal?"

"Oh, that cat? He's inside with grandmother now."

"You're sure?"

She nodded, and the auburn tresses rose and fell like a billowy sea, yet not a hair left its place. "That was very nice of you to give him to grandmother."

"I didn't give her my cat," I snapped. "I loaned him to her for the weekend. Tomorrow afternoon that ten-pound fur ball goes home with me."

"Well, you'll have to take that up with grandmother, I suppose."

"There's no taking up anything, dear. That flea bag is mine."

It's a rare woman that can look stunning *and* stunned at the same time. "Oh, my! Yes, I'm sure he is."

"You bet your bippy, toots." I would have stridden on into the house to see Dmitri for myself, except for two small impediments: one, these legs are incapable of striding, and two, the elegant Alexandra had my arm in a vise grip. Apparently upper-body strength ran in the family.

"Miss Timberlake—do you mind if I call you Abigail?"

"Not if I can call you Andie."

"Miss Timberlake, I know we hardly know each other, but I feel so comfortable talking to you."

"You do?"

"Absolutely. One gets the impression that you are both a sensitive and intelligent person. Surely, you've heard that before."

"All the time," I said. By rights my nose should have grown an inch, and if I were truly my mother's daughter, I would have been overwhelmed by the odor of trouble.

"Well, in that case, do you mind if we talk in the garden? It is so pleasant there this time of the year and besides"—she gestured toward the house—"this is a very personal matter."

"Oh?" I'm a sucker for secrets. I'm good at keeping them, too. For instance, I have yet to divulge whether or not anything happened between me and the president on his last visit to Charlotte.

"Come, we'll talk on the bench." Her tone was not imperious, merely assuming.

I trotted acquiescently after the elegant Alexandra. I had to take two steps for every one of hers.

We sat together on the bench, me cross-legged as before. The river was much higher than it was during my chat with Albert, which meant that alligators were undoubtedly closer. I scanned the water for black "logs."

"Isn't it lovely?" Alexandra said in her patrician accent.

"Yes, ma'am."

She turned, focusing her large orbs on my humble face. "That's such a delightful scent you're wearing. What is it?"

"Desperation," I said. No need to add that it was also the scent of fear, as well as the odor of an unwashed body, a visit to the county jail, and enough garlic lunch to keep even the most voracious of vampires at bay.

"Ah, yes, I believe I've heard of that," she said quite seriously, "I'll have to see if the Dillard's back home carries it."

"I'm sure you can find Desperation at Dillard's, Macy's, Neiman Marcus, you name it. It's in all the better stores."

"Wonderful! I've always said you can tell the status of a woman by the quality of her perfume."

"Oh, is that so?"

"Absolutely."

"Then you might be interested to know that for the past thirty centuries, back to the days of King Solomon, the finest perfumes have used, as a base, oil scooped from the anus of the civet cat." A fact is a fact, after all.

Alexandra's alabaster visage seemed in danger of cracking. "Surely, you're joking."

"I kid you not. But, you didn't bring me here to talk about feline extracts, did you?"

She shook her head slowly.

"So, dear, what's on your mind?"

"Uh—well"—she looked away—"it's not easy for me to talk about."

I may possess the patience of a saint; I just happen to lack a saint's self-control. "Spit it out, dear.

'Time and tide wait for no man,' remember?"

"Miss Timberlake, are you in love with my cousin?"

"*What*?"

She repeated the question, something she richly deserved. But she deserved even more.

"I most certainly am not in love with your cousin, dear. Trust me, Edith is not my type."

"No! I mean Tradd."

"Spare me." Thanks to having raised two teenagers, my derisive snorts rank up there with the best of them. "Tradd Maxwell Burton is of philandering pheromones. I will admit that he lights my fire, so to speak, but a woman would have to be a fool to be in love with him."

"Then I'm a fool," she said quietly.

"You can't be serious!"

"Oh, but I am! I've been in love with Tradd since—well, since we were little children. And he was in love with me, too. We vowed we were going to get married when we grew up. Look over there"—she pointed across the river—"see where the reflection of that old dead tree trunk forms a V? We were going to build our house there."

I patted her alabaster arm. "Isn't that illegal, dear? Marriage between first cousins, I mean."

"Oh, no. It's not illegal in South Carolina." She sighed. "Of course, it takes two to tango, doesn't it?"

"And Tradd wouldn't dance?"

"It was all that hateful floozy Flora's fault. Always laughing and carrying on, mocking me by throwing herself all over Tradd. But, she's dead now, isn't she? Now we'll see who gets the last laugh."

I stole a glance at her long, slender hands. A

well-manicured finger can pull a trigger just as easily as a grubby digit can.

"Did you kill her, dear?"

She stiffened. I may as well have invited her to partake in a belching contest.

"I most certainly did not! Oh, I know, she managed to turn Tradd's head, but it wouldn't have lasted. His infatuation with her, I mean. Class eventually finds its own level, don't you think?"

"Well—"

"Of course, it does. Silly me, then, for worrying about you and Tradd."

"I beg your pardon!"

"No offense intended, Ms. Timberlake. I simply meant that birds of a feather will flock together— that kind of thing. We are cousins, after all. I certainly had no intention of putting you down because you're a merchant. It isn't your fault you weren't born a Latham or a Burton. We can't help our ancestors, now can we? Although these days, what with cloning and all—"

I didn't hear another word of her pathetic prattle. All my senses were tuned to the V she'd pointed out. It hadn't been there at low tide, but now that the shiny black water was high, the single slanted trunk of an ancient tree formed not a V, but an arrow! It had to be. Didn't that quote mention the tide? But, where—the garden shed. The arrow was pointing directly at the dilapidated garden shed. Of course! Everything about gardening was time-related. When to plant, when to water, when to fertilize, when to prune ... gardening and time went hand in hand like Buster and me—I slapped myself for even thinking such a ridiculous thing.

"Mosquito bite you?" Alexandra asked thoughtfully.

"Yeah," I said, thinking as fast as I did that time I absentmindedly walked into the *men*'s room at the Carolina Outlet Mall at Carowinds. Then a cheery "Where's Waldo?" and a quick exit did the trick.

"Funny," Alexandra said, focusing the periwinkle orbs on me again, "but mosquitoes don't usually come out in the heat of the day. Do you think it's because of El Nino?"

I slapped my poor, undeserving cheek again. "Maybe it's just a class thing. Maybe we hoi polloi are sweeter. But, be a doll, dear, and run in and get me some bug screen."

"But wouldn't it make more sense if you got it? I mean, you might get bitten again if you stay here."

"Yes, it would make more sense if I went inside," I said, as slowly as Yankees *think* we talk, "but I'm having an allergic reaction. If I move, it only gets worse."

"Oh, my gosh! This is terrible. Shall I call 911?"

"No need to, sweetie," I drawled. "I keep a vial of antivenom serum in my purse. It's—"

"Your purse is right beside you. There on the bench!"

"Did I say purse? You see, it's happening, already. I meant to say overnight bag. You see, the vial is more like a jar, on account of how allergic I am. It won't fit in this purse."

"Be back in a flash," the dear heart said, and sprinted toward the house.

Fine breeding, indeed! No doubt about it, but if you shook the Latham family tree a Cox would fall out.

The second I heard the house door slam, I sprinted for the garden shed. Why the U.S. Olympic officials don't recruit middle-aged women with a mission, is beyond me. I would have made Carl Lewis bite my dust. At any rate, I flung open the garden shed, willing my eyes to adjust to the dim light. Almost immediately—well before the house door slammed a second time—I saw what I'd come to Georgetown to find. It was all I could do to suppress a scream.

22

"It's the most elaborate Swiss clock I've ever seen," I burbled.

Mrs. Elias Burton Latham III nodded. Dmitri, snuggled safely in the crook of her leathery arms, purred like the works of the finest Swiss clock.

"It's by Emanuel Brugger," the old woman said proudly. "It's even signed by him. And dated—1764. The works are made of beech, you know. Elias and I bought it on our honeymoon."

"I thought you honeymooned in the sultanate of Bandar?"

"Heavens, child, one goes to more than one destination on one's honeymoon! We made a proper grand tour that year. Switzerland was, of course, one of our stops. We picked up the clock in Zurich, in an antique shop that sold a lot of baroque pieces. Elias was very fond of fancy things."

"Look at the detail. The painting. See, these four figures represent the four seasons."

"Exactly. You would have thought that the John Heywood quote would have been a dead giveaway."

I shrugged. "And speaking of dead, this lower

painting—the skull here—symbolizes death."

"Especially Alexandra."

"Come again?"

"It was always one of her favorite things."

"Alexandra Latham has a thing for death?"

The ancient eyes flashed. "Don't be ridiculous. Alexandra was always fond of the clock."

"So, she is familiar with this baroque Swiss clock—"

"Of course, she is. All the grandchildren are. It's been on the mantel in the nursery for over sixty years."

"Wow. And not one of them noticed its absence."

A single tear trickled down a cheek as leathery as Mama's pan-fried steak. "I expected Alexandra to. In fact, I was counting on it. I know one isn't supposed to have favorites, but sometimes it can't be helped."

"You *were*?" I lowered my voice. "Why was it so important that Alexandra find the clock?"

Dmitri squirmed, forcing Mrs. Latham to set him down on her bed. We were in her bedroom, with the door closed. Although I had yet to hear anything suspicious, or see a shadow flicker by the bottom of the door, I just knew someone was out in the hallway. Watching. Listening.

"You see"—the octogenarian said, matching my tone—"there's something hidden here in the back." She slid open a painted wood panel and withdrew a business-size envelope."

"It's not a will, is it?"

She recoiled in surprise. "How did you know?"

"I saw the movie, dear. Or was it some book I read? Anyway, all the ne'er-do-well heirs kill each other trying to find it. Gracious me—"I clapped my hands to my cheeks involuntarily. "Flora Dubois wasn't one of your heirs, was she?"

"Heavens, no! She was my *maid*. And that's all she was. It's a pity though that Tradd couldn't get the picture. Someone had to put a stop to her."

My knees shook. "So *you* killed Flora?"

She sat down heavily on the bed. Unfortunately for poor Dmitri, she sat squarely on his tail. It couldn't have hurt all that bad, the bed was soft, after all, but you would have thought she'd driven an eighteen-wheeler rig over those eight inches of bony fluff.

"Yes, I killed Flora," she said. I didn't actually hear those words, but I'm a fair lip reader. Grandmother Wiggins was as deaf as a turnip.

I waited until my precious ceased his pitiful yowls and was merely hissing. "How did you kill her?" I asked quite sensibly. As far as I knew, Buster had yet to make the details public.

She straightened and raised her chin. "I shot her, of course."

"Where? I mean, what part of her body?"

"Well—okay, but I really had no choice. I shot her in the back of the head."

"I don't suppose firing her was good enough."

"Firing her wouldn't have done anything about the baby. She absolutely refused to get rid of it."

I nodded. "So, you knew about that, too. And you wanted to make doubly sure the little brat wouldn't somehow end up inheriting all this. Well, Mrs. Latham, I think you went to an awful lot of trouble. Why didn't you just give everything to Alexandra now? That's the new thing, you know? Die broke, the experts are saying. That's the only way to go."

"You don't understand," she said. I heard frustration, but not an ounce of remorse. "I wanted the will to be found by someone who loves me. Someone who remembers all the stories I told them in the nursery. About the clock their grandfather and I brought back from our honeymoon. It didn't have to be Alexandra, I was just hoping it was."

It was time to put away the violins; a woman was dead, after all. Even strumpets deserved to be avenged.

"Tell that to Flora's parents," I said sharply. "Tell that to someone who really cares." I eyed the distance to the door. Unless she had the gun hidden in her bra, and was one hell of a quick draw, I was assured of a safe getaway. "You know, of course, I'm going to have to turn you in."

"I'm fully aware of that," she said flatly.

I took several steps backward. "And just because you played with God as a child, doesn't mean they're going to let you off the hook."

She actually smiled. "I'm eighty-nine. I could use a rest."

Two more steps. "South Carolina has the death penalty, you know."

She had the audacity to laugh. "I've had a heart condition for the past ten years. How much longer would I live, anyway?"

"But what about C.J.!" I wailed. "Don't you give a damn about her? Don't you understand that you're ruining her life?"

"Nonsense, child. Neely Thompson and our young coroner—Buster, they call him—are no fools. By now they must have discovered that Flora wasn't stabbed to death. But what she was doing with the sultan's kris is beyond me. Anyway, I doubt that a few hours in jail will have ruined her life. After all, she isn't one of us."

"One of *us*? Just what is that supposed to mean? Look, C.J. may be an egg or two short of an Easter basket, but she has feelings."

The dowager waved a biscuit hand. "Don't get me wrong, I find the girl delightful. But girls of her class don't have that much to lose, now do they?"

"Her *class*?"

She nodded. "Now, you—that's a different story. I can tell that you come from a good family. And Timberlake—Bob Timberlake is a famous North Carolina artist, isn't he? So, you married well, too."

"I didn't marry Bob," I screamed, "I married Buford. They're no relation. And Buford has about as much class as you do! No, I guess he has a trifle more, because he has yet to kill anybody."

One giant step backward and I was at the door. Dmitri, however, had decided to forgive the doting dowager and had curled up on her pillow.

"Dmitri! Come to mama!"

My fickle friend opened one eye.

I turned the knob and gave the door a push. "Now!"

My feckless feline closed his eye. A satin pillow and someone to cater to his every whim, versus a fur-covered blanket in a wicker kitty basket and an owner too busy to even keep track of her shadow, much less a cat, what was there to choose?

"Traitor!" I shrieked, and stepping backward into the hall, pulled her heavy door shut.

I didn't even have a chance to turn around. The blow to the back of my head came as a total surprise. And that's when the lights went out in Georgetown.

I awoke in degrees. Bright flashes of color and intense pain alternating with darkness and an overwhelming need to sleep. Gradually the colors dimmed, and I became more alert, but my surroundings were still as dark as Tweetie Bird's roots. The pain, incidentally, never left me. I felt like the Carolina Panthers were using my head to practice kicking field goals.

After dozens of kicks—most of them undoubtedly winners—I began to feel the sensation of movement. Short, hard jerks that coincided with the field goals. Apparently I was locked inside something. Possibly a large box of some kind.

"Hey, let me out!"

"Not on your life," someone said and laughed. The jerking continued.

I will admit I entertained the idea that I might be dead and was, in fact, in hell—but the thought lasted only a few seconds, mind you. I am an Episcopalian, after all. For us hell is having to use plastic cutlery at a tailgate party.

"Let me out now!"

"You're a fiery little thing, I'll give you that."

"*Albert*?"

"Hell, I guess it doesn't really matter if you know it's me. You're not going to live long enough to do anything about it."

"Albert Jansen! You let me out, right this minute. Did Edith put you up to this?"

"Edith—that's a laugh!"

Before I could ask what was so funny, the box, or whatever it was that contained me, pitched forward and fell a good two feet. My lights flickered again as all eleven Carolina Panthers kicked me simultaneously. You can bet your bippy I screamed like there was no tomorrow.

Albert pounded on my prison. "Shut up!"

"Make me, you idiot! What did you do, drop me off a cliff?"

"I dropped you in Grandmother Latham's rowboat. You're a hell of a lot heavier than you look."

Sure enough, I could feel myself rocking. "Ninety-eight pounds soaking wet, you wuss. Edith could sling me over her shoulder with one hand. Besides, this box has got to weigh a ton."

"I'm not a wuss, and this isn't a box. It's a chest."

"Ah, the one with all the lifesavers and junk."

"That's the one. But it's empty now, except for you."

But if I recalled correctly, it was no ordinary chest. I had only ever seen two of them before. Both Bavarian-made, and both intended to serve double duty as chest and cradle. *Kinderkaschete* they were called. If a small child was inadvertently trapped inside, they merely needed to slide open a ventilation panel. And I, as I've been reminded far too often, am barely larger than a small child.

"You ready to take a little boat ride?" Albert called.

"Not until I've got a lifesaver on, dear. It's the law, you know."

"It isn't where you're going."

He had pushed off from the dock and I could hear the faint splash of oars. "And where might that be?"

"First out to the middle of the Black River, and then straight down to the bottom."

"Why, that's stupid," I said stupidly. "Out in the middle of the river folks are going to see you." I tried to slap my face in the darkness of the trunk, and ended up banging my elbow.

"Oh, there's a little detail I forgot to mention," Albert said, putting his face sadistically close to the lid, "but it's night now.. A nice, dark moonless night."

"But, that's impossible!"

"You were out a long time, Abigail. Stashed safely away in the attic. Of course, everyone else thinks you've gone home. That's what I told them, you see. I told them you said you had had enough of the Burton-Latham clan. I told them you called a cab."

Try to keep your assailant talking—I'd heard that on *Oprah* or some other talk show. "There really is no need for this, dear. The old lady confessed to everything. Surely, you heard that. You were waiting right outside her door."

"Yeah, I heard all right. She was weak."

"So, you were in this together?"

"Not hardly. She killed Flora, not me."

"Then why are you doing this to me?"

"Like I said, Grandmother Latham is weak. She's bound to talk sooner or later."

"What's it to you if she talks?" I screamed. "She killed Flora, not you."

"Oh, but I was there."

"You saw it?"

"I was *there*."

"Repetition is the cardinal law of learning, dear, but with you, I'm afraid it's a sign of senility."

"I was *with* Flora. Flora and I were lovers."

"Oh." It was no doubt unproductive to point out that Flora and half the male population of Georgetown County were lovers.

"The old bag came downstairs in the storm expecting to find Tradd. Under other circumstances it might have been funny. I certainly didn't expect her to shoot Flora."

"Pow. Right in the back of the head," I said. If

he couldn't be overcome by guilt, maybe gore would do the trick.

"Yeah, pow. But then she had this witness, see? And I had this major problem."

"Ah, yes, her money. You're afraid she's going to tell Edith, who will drop you like a hot potato. Then it's bye-bye big bucks."

"You're a smart woman, Abigail. I would have enjoyed being married to someone like you."

"In your dreams, dear."

He let my sarcasm roll off him, like black water from a gator. "Anyway, for a minute, I thought the old crone was going to shoot me, too. You should have seen the look on her face! But, fortunately, your fruity friend came into the kitchen—" He stopped talking, and I heard the faint splash of paddles again. "Middle of the river."

"That's nice, dear, but finish your story. So, C.J. came along, carrying the kris for protection and—"

"And—over you go!"

My lights barely flickered when I hit the water. What came as a shock was how quickly the chest began to take on water. Apparently Mrs. Latham neglected to put the boathouse on her annual termite-inspection list. Nonetheless, it was imperative that I wait until Albert had seen the chest sink out of sight. So, although it was one of the hardest things I've ever done, I stayed put until the water sloshed into my nostrils. The trapdoor opened easily, and just as easily I slipped out and into the cool black water.

To be honest, I didn't have time to be scared. Besides, I'm a decent swimmer, thanks to all those afternoons spent at the Fort Mill water park when Buford and I were courting. Buford, who was over a foot taller than me, was so dazzled by my charms that he never noticed me treading water in places where he could easily stand.

At any rate, the Black River in summer is delightfully warm. Much warmer, if you ask me, than the water at Myrtle Beach. But Albert was right—it most definitely was night. Had it not been for the lights of the Latham house in the distance, the water, the shore, and the sky would have all blended together. I couldn't even see Albert in the boat.

I listened for the slap of oars against the surface. Nothing. Perhaps he was sitting motionless in the boat waiting. The man was an engineer, after all; they're sticklers for details.

Then something brushed against my foot. Something that might have been a fish, or a piece of wood, or an *alligator*. I broke the world's record for free-style swimming getting to shore.

23

"And then what happened?" Mama asked.

She'd come down to pick up C.J. and me, and Buster's aunt, bless her soul, had invited her to lunch, as well. Why on earth our hostess had to include C.J. *and* both Triplett brothers is beyond me. What's more, Buster didn't seem to mind one bit.

"Well, then I sneaked into the house—taking great care to avoid the grande dame, of course— and told the entire story to Edith. She was very helpful."

"She wasn't mad because you killed her husband?" C.J. really should remember to swallow her food before speaking.

"Abby!" Mama dropped her fork and her hand flew to her pearls. "You killed Albert?"

"Of course, not, Mama. Albert drowned when he threw me overboard. He lost his balance and the boat tipped over. Apparently he had never learned to swim. Besides, the boat was leaking so fast, he didn't have a chance anyway."

Buster's Aunt Amelia handed me a large bowl of mashed potatoes. They were the homemade kind, heavy with butter and cream. Even Mama would be hard pressed to make better.

"My nephew Floyd, here, was a swimming champion in high school," she said pointedly.

C.J. popped another bite of pot roast in her mouth. "I thought your name was Buster."

I gave C.J. a warning look. "It is. Buster is his middle name."

"I have a cousin Floyd—"

I cut off her off at the pass. "Turns out Edith Jansen is a pretty nice woman. She just comes across strong with outsiders because she's trying to protect her family. As soon as she called the sheriff she marched right into her grandmother's room and rescued Dmitri for me."

"Considering that Flora is dead," Daniel Triplett said solemnly, "Edith should have protected outsiders *from* her family."

"So," Mama said, picking up her fork, "everyone in the family suspected Mrs. Latham had hidden her will in that fancy clock?"

"They *knew* she'd hidden it in the missing piece, they just didn't know what that piece was. But nobody knew the terms of the will—except Flora. She was the old bag's witness."

Mama poked me with her fork. "Abby, how you talk!"

"Sorry," I looked first to Mama, and then Buster's Aunt Amelia. Of course, neither of them were anywhere near eighty-nine.

"So, what were the terms?" Buster asked.

"I know, I know," C.J. said waving both arms. "She left everything to Alexandra, didn't she?"

"Yes and no."

"It can't be both, Abby."

"Yes, it can. You see—"

"But, maybe you're right. There's a building in Shelby that is the world's shortest skyscraper and—"

"Excuse me," Mama said, and stretching across Aunt Amelia's broad table poked C.J. with her fork. "Let Abby finish her story."

"Well, like I was about to say, the will divided everything equally between all four grandchildren—the children themselves were left entirely out—but there was a codicil that stated the entire will was null and void if Alexandra found it first. If that was the case, the old—I mean, Mrs. Latham—was going to have a new will drawn up leaving everything to the lass with the auburn locks."

"Is that legal?" Buster asked turning to Rhett.

"We'd have to look it up," Daniel said, saving his brother the trouble of rasping. "We lawyers rely heavily on books."

"And legal assistants who have to comb through the books," Rhett said anyway. By the way C.J. was making goo-goo eyes at him, he must have deduced she found his voice charming.

Aunt Amelia nudged me with a veritable vat of gravy. "I've known Genevieve Latham's grandchildren since they were born—they came to visit her just about every summer. Anyway, I must say I'm shocked at the way young Rupert turned out. That shaved head, and all. Are you sure he didn't have anything to do with the maid's murder?"

"Positive." I passed the gravy to Mama. "By the way," I whispered, "you might be interested in knowing that Toy no longer parks cars for Fallen Stars."

"Oh, I know," Mama said, just as calm as could be. "He hasn't worked there in over a year."

"*What?*" Of course everyone looked my way.

"Abby's brother Toy is becoming an Episcopal priest," Mama announced proudly.

"*What*? Mama is this supposed to be a joke? I mean, you would have told me long before this, if it was true."

"This is no joke, dear. Your brother is in the top 10 percent of his class at seminary."

"But Toy's a ne'er-do-well," I wailed. "A sower of wild oats. A prodigal son!"

"I knew you'd say that, Abby. That's why I never told you. It's a shame you and your brother never communicate."

"I bet y'all don't have that problem," C.J. cooed to Rhett.

Aunt Amelia mercifully distracted me with a tureen of green beans and fatback. "Buster said you'd help him pick out a few good pieces. Personally, I'd pick that highboy over there. I think it's worth a pretty penny."

"It's a beautiful piece," I said, feeling put on the spot. I'd noticed the highboy the minute I walked into the house—noticed that it was a reproduction, as were most of Aunt Amelia's "antiques." But the dear lady had graciously allowed me to bring Dmitri into her house, and he reposed at that very moment on my lap, beneath the tablecloth.

"My Abby knows her stuff," Mama said proudly.

C.J. unglued her eyes from Rhett. "You never did say, Abby. Did you get to keep that eighteenth-century Swiss baroque clock?"

I shook my head. "The old lady—I mean, Mrs. Latham, reneged on her promise. She never intended for anyone but Alexandra to have it, and now—well, I've torn her family apart, haven't I?"

"There, there," Mama patted my arm for a

change instead of her pearls. "You don't need to worry about losing out on some dumb clock."

"That clock would have sold at auction for over two hundred thousand dollars."

"Is that all?" She sounded positively cheerful.

The phone rang.

"I'll get it," Buster said to his aunt, who was busy trying to tuck a silver-plated serving spoon into a heaping bowl of collard greens.

Buster was back in a Mississippi minute, which is even longer than a Carolina minute. "It's your boyfriend," he said to me.

"I don't have a boyfriend," I snapped.

Buster frowned. "Someone named Craig Washburn?"

"That's Greg, and he is *not* my boyfriend."

His face relaxed. "That's what he said you'd say. He also said you weren't likely to take his call."

"He was right about that."

"So, he said to give you a message."

I waggled my eyebrows. "Not *here*," I muttered.

Buster was a bust at reading faces. "He said to tell you they found the contents of your shop."

I stood up, spilling Dmitri on the floor. "They *what*?"

He put a strong, warm hand on my arm. "I'm afraid it's not good news, Abby. The truck the thieves were driving overturned on I-40 in the mountains west of Asheville. According to Craig— I mean, Greg—the contents of the truck were pretty much pulverized. But, one of the thieves confessed."

I felt faint. This bit of news was the final nail in the coffin that had been my career. "Fat lot of good a confession does," I said bitterly.

"Well, at least it's closure, isn't it?" C.J. said.

"And don't worry, Abby. I can loan you some money. I've got oodles saved." To her credit, she was just trying to be helpful.

"Forget it, dear, it's over."

"No, it isn't!" Mama grabbed my arm and squeezed it hard. "Remember that angel I showed you, Abby?"

"*Pleeeeease*," I wailed. "I saw you make a fool of yourself on TV—"

"Well, this fool," Mama said, squeezing harder, "charged thirty thousand people ten dollars each to see that angel. Abby, dear, you're rich."

"You're joking," I said, and fainted. Not a mere swoon, mind you, but an out-and-out dead faint.

If it weren't for Mama's grip, and the surprisingly strong arms of Buster, I would have slid under the tablecloth to join Dmitri.

DEN OF ANTIQUITY MYSTERIES

by
TAMAR MYERS

LARCENY AND OLD LACE
78239-1/$5.99 US/$7.99 Can

As owner of the Den of Antiquity, Abigail Timberlake
is accustomed to navigating the cutthroat world of rival
dealers at flea markets and auctions. But she never thought
she'd be putting her expertise in mayhem and detection to
other use—until her aunt was found murdered . . .

GILT BY ASSOCIATION
78237-5/$5.99 US/$7.99 Can

A superb gilt-edged, 18th-century French armoire Abigail
purchased for a song at estate auction has just arrived
along with something she didn't pay for: a dead body.

THE MING AND I
79255-9/$5.99 US/$7.99 Can

Digging up old family dirt can uncover long buried
secrets . . . and a new reason for murder.

SO FAUX, SO GOOD
79254-0/$5.99 US/$7.99 Can

IRIS HOUSE B & B MYSTERIES
by
JEAN HAGER

Featuring Proprietress and part-time sleuth, Tess Darcy

SEW DEADLY
78638-9/$5.99 US/$7.99 Can

THE LAST NOEL
78637-0/$5.99 US/$7.99 Can

DEATH ON THE DRUNKARD'S PATH
77211-6/$5.50 US/$7.50 Can

DEAD AND BURIED
77210-8/$5.50 US/$7.50 Can

A BLOOMING MURDER
77209-4/$5.50 US/$7.50 Can